Nick's superb third-grade book report on Rush Revere!

Also in the Adventures of Rush Revere series

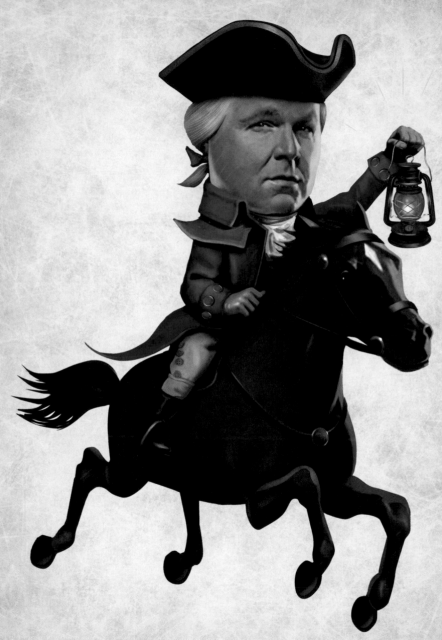

Shining the light on history

Rush Revere
and the
STAR-SPANGLED
BANNER

*Time-Travel Adventures with
Exceptional Americans*

RUSH
LIMBAUGH

with Kathryn Adams Limbaugh

Historical Consultant: Jonathan Adams Rogers
Children's Writing Consultant: Chris Schoebinger
Illustrations by Christopher Hiers

THRESHOLD EDITIONS

NEW YORK   LONDON   TORONTO   SYDNEY   NEW DELHI

Threshold Editions
An Imprint of Simon & Schuster, Inc.
1230 Avenue of the Americas
New York, NY 10020

First Threshold Editions hardcover edition October 2015

THRESHOLD EDITIONS and colophon are trademarks of Simon & Schuster, Inc.

For information about special discounts for bulk purchases, please contact Simon & Schuster Special Sales at 1-866-506-1949 or business@simonandschuster.com.

The Simon & Schuster Speakers Bureau can bring authors to your live event. For more information or to book an event, contact the Simon & Schuster Speakers Bureau at 1-866-248-3049 or visit our website at www.simonspeakers.com.

Manufactured in the United States of America

10 9 8 7 6 5 4 3 2 1

Library of Congress Cataloging-in-Publication Data is available.

ISBN 978-1-4767-8988-0
ISBN 978-1-4767-8992-7 (ebook)

This book is dedicated to Kit Carson and
our irreplaceable friends and family
who faced terrible illnesses over these past years.
They battled heroically with smiles reminding us how precious life is.
They, and so many of you in similar circumstances
are the definition of courage.
God bless you.

Betsy Ross, creator of the first American flag.

Angelyna, a special young adventurer.

Foreword

We live in an incredible country that we are privileged to call home. America is a country to be honored, revered, and appreciated. It is unique. There is no place like America. It is the one country in the history of mankind where the citizens are protected from an overreaching government. We have no king. We have no dictator. We choose those who will govern and lead us. Our founding documents are based on the concepts of individual liberty. America is a phenomenon precisely because of this commitment to freedom. But America is not perfect. No country is, because there is no such thing as perfect.

I love America, and I stand in awe of those who founded it, created it, defend it, and protect it more and more as I grow older. Our country is young by many measures, but our history is rich! There are endless examples and lessons in our history that may serve as a guide for the future. My hope is to rekindle the American patriotic spirit, the love of country, and have it carry on for generations to come. The early patriots who wrote and created some of the most important documents ever, the Constitution and Bill of Rights, were true geniuses. That they could craft concepts, guidelines, and laws for our country that would stand for centuries, concepts that had never been codified in any other land before, is nothing short of a miracle.

The American flag is iconic, a symbol of our freedom and strength as a nation. Every time I see the red, white, and blue stripes waving in the wind at a stadium or being escorted into an event by military personnel, my heart skips beats. Sometimes my eyes tear up. Other times I stand and cheer. Those colors, stars, and stripes represent so much, including sacrifices made by so many before us.

We know that the United States and the early exceptional patriots faced numerous challenges and hardships along the way—hardships we can only imagine today. The founding, building, and formation of our country was not easy, and it took a great deal of patience, wisdom, courage, faith, and inner strength to persevere.

While we can only imagine the physical hardships our early patriots endured, that is not to say we necessarily have it easier. Life is full of difficult periods, and it always will be. There are times when inexplicable darkness seems to block the light for a period of time. In this past year, I watched dear friends and family face extraordinarily difficult medical circumstances. There was nothing fair about it and the pain was, at times, unbearable.

Sometimes bad things happen to good people. And just like the early American patriots, these friends and family were so brave and determined through it all, relying heavily on their faith and their families and friends. In many cases, it was the grandparents who possessed the knowledge and wisdom of long lives who helped the children to cope with and understand why these tragedies occurred.

They all reminded me just how special and precious life is, how lucky we are to have all that we have as Americans, and how each day is truly a gift. They wanted the best for their children and for future generations, as I do. The United States of America offers that opportunity to be the best, discover the best and live the best life possible.

Rush Revere and crew are ready to go meet more exceptional Americans. So hold on tight . . . and let's *rush, rush, rush to history*!

Prologue

Shouting and yells could be heard in the distant blackness. Washington City was barely visible as Liberty and I made our way down a winding dirt road.

"Liberty, I hope you can see better than I can," I said. "I forgot there are no street lights in 1814."

"No worries, Revere. Horses can see very well in the dark," Liberty said. "And I can smell better, too. Well, not just in the dark but all the time. In fact," Liberty sniffed, "it smells like someone is cooking dinner. Mmm, a nice carrot and onion stew sounds really—whoa!" Liberty yelled and reared up, flailing his front legs.

The sound of a woman screaming came from somewhere directly in front of us.

I hung tight to Liberty's neck until his front hooves were once again on the dirt road. "What was that all about," I said.

"Sorry, but those people spooked me. I didn't see them until the last second," Liberty replied.

"I thought you could see well in the dark," I said with sarcasm.

"I can. But I had my eyes closed when I was smelling that delicious . . . oh, never mind. We have company," whispered Liberty.

A woman and toddler briskly walked to the other side of the road, moving fast and away from us and the city. They appeared to be carrying their household belongings. Both were covered in dirt and looked exhausted.

"Are you okay?" I asked, concerned. "I'm sorry my horse spooked you."

"All is well, thank you," the woman replied. "We are tired but we are faring as well as possible under the circumstances."

The young girl beside her looked to be around seven years old with long brown hair and a high-collared dress. Her tired eyes brightened when she saw Liberty. "Your horse is so pretty!" she exclaimed. "Can I pet his nose?"

"Of course you may. He loves that almost as much as he loves carrots," I said.

Liberty leaned down and snuggled into the girl's nose.

"You are very kind, sir," the woman said in a weary tone. "Please be careful. The British are on the edge of the city. We were told to evacuate. There are rumors that four thousand Redcoats are marching toward Washington. They plan to burn the city in revenge for their defeat at York."

"Thank you for the warning. We will be on the lookout," I replied, putting a hand to the edge of my tricornered hat to bid them farewell.

"Bye-bye, horsey," the little girl said as they walked away into the dark night.

"Revere, I thought we were going to see the White House," Liberty said, as we pressed forward on the dusty road.

"We are, but I'm a bit disoriented," I replied. I looked down at my map of Washington City in 1814. The Capitol was being built, and the White House is where it still stands today in Washington, D.C. On August 23, 1814, however, the city was still under construction. As we continued to walk we noticed building materials all along the road.

"I think I can help," said Liberty. "After all, I do have Spidey-sense for all things American history." Liberty paused, closed his eyes, and sniffed the air.

"Well?" I asked. "Which way do we go?"

"I don't know," Liberty said. "The only thing I'm getting is the smell of roasted vegetables and boy, does it smell good!"

I rolled my eyes. "Look over there," I said. "I think that's the dome of the Capitol Building. We're almost there."

After a few minutes, we arrived at our destination. The light from nearby torches reflected off the white walls of the White House. We picked up our pace as we approached. There was nothing around the building except a road in front and dirt and grass surrounding it. A small gate was left open and we were able to enter the grounds without being stopped.

A man approached us carrying small items. "President Madison has already left, sir, and I suggest you do the same," the man said as he brushed past.

"I am starting to think the same thing, Revere," Liberty said. "Except that delicious smell is coming from the White House. I'm sure of it. Maybe they're expecting us for dinner?"

"Liberty, our mission is to find Dolley Madison, the First Lady."

"Right, I know," said Liberty. "I'm just saying if she invites us to dinner it would be rude to say no."

"It's true that Dolley Madison was said to be an incredible hostess, but that's not why we're here."

As we turned a corner behind the White House we saw two men helping a woman roll up a large canvas painting. I knew it was the rare and priceless portrait of George Washington by Gilbert Stuart.

"That's her!" I exclaimed. "The First Lady of the United States of America."

As we approached I saw Dolley place the rolled-up portrait into the hands of a young African-American man.

"You there, come help us with this painting," Mrs. Madison said. I knew it was the First Lady because I had studied a painting of her before we left modern day. She had dark hair, dark eyes, and pale skin. She continued to dart back and forth as she gathered and boxed other documents.

"Yes, Mrs. Madison," I said, "we are certainly happy to help."

"Thank you," she said. "Help us roll this painting so that it is not damaged."

I jumped off Liberty and helped the others carefully roll the giant canvas.

"The President has gone to the battlefield, and everyone is exhausted. I thank you for your help. I suspect the British will be here soon to destroy Washington City, so we are removing the items that are most valuable to the country. It is a small thing, perhaps, but I think it is important," Mrs. Madison said.

"Why is the portrait of George Washington so important?" I asked.

Dolley Madison saved George Washington's portrait during the burning of Washington in 1814. She is seen here.

"Because if the British are able to take the painting of George Washington, the hero of the Revolution and the namesake of this city, they will be able to say they have defeated us, both physically and mentally."

Mrs. Madison took a deep breath and exhaled. "This feels like the longest day of my life," she said. "I suppose some may say this is ridiculous, but it is more than a painting. It is a sacred symbol of our freedom, and I cannot leave it to be destroyed by the British."

As she spoke, she moved quickly through the grounds and back into the White House. I followed her, nearly out of breath as she moved quickly from room to room.

"Ask her about dinner," whispered Liberty as I walked out of the White House, carrying a small, heavy chest.

As if she heard Liberty, Mrs. Madison replied, "Unfortunately, I was expecting a party of forty dinner guests tonight. The table is set, the food prepared, and now it will be wasted on those British Lobsterbacks!"

She sighed as she looked at her home, and said, "It is done. My carriage awaits on the other side of the White House. Do not delay your departure, Mr. Revere. I understand the British are boasting that if I am captured they will parade me through the streets of London as a prisoner."

"Thank you so much, Mrs. Madison," I said. "Godspeed." We went our separate ways and I went outside to find Liberty.

"Did you save the food?" asked Liberty in desperation.

"Seriously?" I said. "You're worried about food when the city is about to be torched and the First Lady is trying to avoid capture by the British?"

Liberty shrugged.

"Okay, Mr. Grumpypants. Let's head back to modern day and get you fed. We need to gather the Crew.

"Aye, aye, Captain Starve-a-Horse," Liberty said. "Just give me a second while I muster up enough strength to open the time portal."

I laughed and reached into Liberty's saddlebag for two apples, a large carrot, and a cup of oats.

Once Liberty finished his pre-jumping snack, I climbed up onto his saddle and said, "Rush, rush, rush from history!"

At that, the time portal opened, spinning in yellow and purple, and we jumped through to modern day.

Chapter 1

*L*iberty *and I* walked through a spacious park with
tall trees that looked like large bouquets of orange
and yellow leaves. On this early fall morning, the grass was
still green and the birds chirped in harmony. There was a
slight cool breeze and the air was cool as we made our way
closer to the hospital.

"Look, that must be it!" Liberty said looking across the
street. His mane was waving gently in the wind.

"Way to go, Liberty. Sharp eye," I said. Up ahead, a large
American flag waved outside the main entrance of the Veterans' Hospital. The red, white, and blue colors stood out
vibrantly against the overcast sky. It was as if the flag was
standing guard.

"Do I get a treat for being right? I mean that really does
seem to be the right thing to do. Don't you think?" Liberty
asked. Food was never far from his mind. Instead of a

snack here and there, Liberty preferred a snack here, there, and everywhere.

I purposely left the first question hanging, but a second soon followed. "By the way, when are we eating lunch?" asked Liberty.

"It's not even ten o'clock in the morning," I said. "Have a carrot."

"I ate all my carrots," Liberty whined.

"Then have an apple," I insisted.

"I ate all my apples, too," Liberty said, with a shrug.

"Are you joking around?" I asked. I poked inside Liberty's saddlebag for something tasty, but there was nothing. "I thought I saw you eating a bunch of grains this morning," I said.

Liberty rolled his eyes. "Of course I ate my grains. But you know I'm a very active horse. I burn calories like a race car burns rubber. Do you know how much fuel it takes to launch the space shuttle into orbit? Well, I take a lot of fuel, too, jumping back in time."

I sighed and stifled a laugh. Liberty was right. Ever since we first met, Liberty and I have been time-traveling buddies. I teach history and Liberty uses his magic to take us to fun places in American history.

"Hello, earth to Rush Revere. Come in, Rush Revere," chattered Liberty. I was lost in thought, remembering how a lightning storm blasted Liberty from the eighteenth century to modern day.

"I can hear you," I said, reaching into my pocket and pulling out a breath mint. "Here, suck on this. It's all I have."

"A breath mint? Oh, lucky me. One whole breath mint. I'm stuffed."

"Smart aleck," I mumbled.

On the way up the driveway, I stopped and asked Liberty to stand by a tree while I went inside.

"Here's the plan," I said. "I am going inside the hospital to speak with Tommy."

"What is Tommy doing at the hospital? Is he sick?" asked Liberty.

Tommy was one of my first students to experience Liberty's time-traveling ability. He visited the Pilgrims on the *Mayflower* with us in the year 1620.

"Tommy texted last night and said he really wanted to speak with me. He said his grandfather is very ill and they admitted him to the hospital. Unfortunately, horses are not allowed inside. Could you wait here for a bit and not get into trouble?"

"Sure thing, no problem. Say hello to Tommy and tell him that I miss him," Liberty said. Then he sheepishly added, "And if, by chance, you walk by the snack shop, could you please bring me a treat? Preferably something *bigger* than a breath mint."

I shook my head and smiled. "I promise I'll get you some food as soon as I finish speaking with Tommy. I'll be back soon."

Liberty nodded with a little grin and looked curiously around the park.

I looked down at the buttons on my coat. Knowing that I planned to visit a hospital with combat veterans, I made sure to burnish the buttons on my blue colonial jacket. Also, I shined my black boots and cleaned and ironed my brown knee britches. If someone didn't know any better, they would think I was from the year 1776. My students learned best, I thought, when they saw me in colonial dress.

With a deep breath I walked through the hospital's sliding doors. A security guard asked me to remove my tricorner hat so he could take my photograph. He then handed me a printed identification badge and pointed me down the hall.

"Just take the elevator to the second floor. The room you're looking for is past the nurses' station on your left," the guard said.

Everything was white and smelled like cleaning solution as I walked down a long hallway. Parked wheelchairs and transport beds lined both sides. Doctors and nurses passed by, wearing white lab coats and light blue surgery scrubs, most looking at their notes.

On the second floor, I exited the elevator and followed the numbers until I reached room 224. I knocked softly and slowly pushed open the door.

I saw Tommy sitting at the side of a hospital bed, floppy blond hair around his ears. He was almost a shadow against the large window.

"Hello, Tommy," I whispered.

At first he didn't hear me, looking deep in thought. His back was hunched and both hands were holding up his chin. A foot-ball rested right beside him on the corner of the bed.

Moving closer, I tried again, "Hi, buddy . . ."

Then to my side, a tall blond man approached. He reached out his hand to shake mine and whispered, "My name is Hank. I'm Tommy's dad. You must be Mr. Revere." He wore a button-down checked shirt tucked into jeans with loafers.

Upon hearing my name, Tommy turned around and said in a low voice, "Hi, Mr. Revere." The room was chilly, with sterile white walls. Several machines beeped and churned rhythmi-cally.

"Hi, Tommy, how are you?" I asked. As I came farther into the room I noticed a man resting on the hospital bed.

"I'm okay," he said, but his face looked pale. "I'm glad you're here."

"I'm happy to be here," I said, softly.

"Mr. Revere, I would like to introduce you to Tommy's grandfather. He is resting now but he can hear what we are saying," Hank said.

I walked closer to the bedside and said, "It is a pleasure to meet you, sir."

Behind Tommy's grandfather in a ray of sunlight was a small gathering of framed photos. I recognized Tommy and his grandfather in one photograph, throwing a football outside. Beside it was an old photo of a man in military uniform. In front of both photos, a small American flag pin rested on a small wooden box.

The room was generally quiet, apart from the occasional beep of the heart monitor and nurses chatting in the hallway.

Hank filled the void, saying, "If Tommy's grandfather had enough energy to speak with you, he would probably grab you around the shoulders and shake you to say hello. Also, he would probably quiz you about your hat selection and your adventures in history. Maybe a little later, after he has rested."

I smiled and nodded.

Tommy added, "Grandpa loves watching football in his den. He has this big chair that no one else can sit in. Sometimes Dad tries to sneak in and sit there before he does, but not for long. Grandpa says, 'Move it, Hank!' He knows every player better than the announcers. He says things like, *That's John Sanders from Ohio State, his mother is a teacher.* He totally knows everything about sports."

"Yes, he does for sure," Hank said smiling.

Tommy continued: "Remember during halftime when Grandpa would grab hot chocolate in mugs and we would go out in the snow? You played center, Dad, and I played quarterback. Grandpa would either play defense or would go out for a pass. Remember, he always wore the same brown sweater with a hole in the sleeve and pretended he had a bad back until he snuck up and tackled me to the ground?"

Hank laughed, and looked down at his father on the bed. Tommy's grandfather seemed to be smiling in his rest.

"The best is he taught me how to throw a spiral," Tommy remembered, picking up the football lying near his grandfather's leg. "One year he spent the whole summer teaching me how to throw the perfect spiral. For some reason, I just couldn't get it, and threw a duck again and again. Grandpa would laugh but would say, 'Don't worry, it will come in its time, just keep practicing.' Eventually, after trying again and again and again, the ball went from flopping through the air, to an awesome spinning spiral. It was really cool."

"I remember that, too, Tommy," Hank said.

"I wish we could throw the ball right now," Tommy said, looking somberly out the window toward the near-empty parking lot.

Hank followed his gaze and said, "Tommy, why don't you and Mr. Revere take a walk down the hall for a bit? You've been in this room a long time."

"That sounds like a good idea," I agreed. "I would love to catch up and hear what's been happening with you."

Tommy asked, "Is Liberty here?"

"Yes, he's out in the front of the hospital. He wanted to come in and see you but I thought he had better stay outside. I told him it was a hospital, not a *horse*-pital," I joked softly, hoping to lift the mood just a little. Tommy was usually such a jokester.

Tommy gave my effort a half smile and made his way toward the door, gripping the football to his side. I nodded to Tommy's father, indicating that I would speak with him more later.

Tommy seemed to really know his way around the hospital halls, even though they all looked exactly the same to me. He led us right to the family waiting room and grabbed two open seats. At first he didn't say anything, just slumped in his seat, head down, with his hands in his pockets.

"I'm impressed you know exactly where the soda machine is. Great job," I said, not sure how to begin.

"My grandpa is really sick. I can tell the doctor is worried," Tommy said, staring straight at the floor. "They are still doing some tests."

I looked at him closely and eventually his eyes caught mine. Every time I saw Tommy in class or on our time-travel adventures I became more and more impressed with his ability to shift from class clown to sincere student. He was an athlete—quarterback of the Manchester Lions football team—but he also had a softness and profound intelligence.

"I'm sorry to hear your grandfather is not well. He's fighting a difficult battle right now," I said. I did not know all the details, but I wanted to comfort him.

Tommy nodded. "My grandpa's a fighter. He played tight end for his football team, and he had his nose broken like three times. But he said he always laughed it off. He knew that getting tackled was just part of the job." Tommy took a sip of his soda and without looking up, continued his thoughts. "Oh, and he's a real hero, too. He went on these helicopters in Vietnam, and there was a lot of shooting. But he didn't really like to talk about the scary stuff much. Sometimes he would start and then say, 'Tommy, let's talk about fun stuff like the game this weekend.'"

I knew the best thing to do was listen as Tommy shared bits and pieces of stories about his grandfather. One memory led to another. After about a half an hour, the waiting room seats became uncomfortable so we stood up to look out the window.

"Is that Liberty?" Tommy asked, with a full smile. Sure enough, Liberty was far below between some trees and it looked like he was practicing his dance moves. Tommy and I both started laughing.

"Yep, that's Liberty," I said, smiling.

Dark, puffy clouds crept across the sky like a curtain closing on a stage. The sun's rays reached out as if holding one final pose and then bowed to the darkness and the generous applause of rain.

In the midst of a sad occasion, Liberty had made Tommy smile, and I was happy about that. We finally figured out that Liberty, for some reason, was trying to dodge the raindrops falling around him.

"You know, Tommy, there are difficult times in life, just like this storm. One minute everything seems fine, and the next we are running for cover just like Liberty down there."

The brown speck below darted left and then right and then left again. Finally, Liberty bolted for shelter near the front of the hospital.

I breathed deeply and said, "In these times, it's normal to not really know what to do. And that's okay," I said, putting my hand on his shoulder.

At that moment, a blur of red and blue caught my eye. The

flag we saw on the way in was waving and fighting against the storm and the wind. But it was flying strong. Goose bumps went up my arms.

"I just want Grandpa to be okay. He's got to wake up and get out of here. He just has to," Tommy said, shrugging his shoulders.

"I know, Tommy. You are being so brave."

"Really? I don't think I'm brave, but Grandpa is. He probably learned that in the military, I don't know, but he is really tough," Tommy said.

As mature and smart as Tommy was for his age, I knew he could use a little break from everything. I asked him if he was ready to head back and see his father and grandfather and he said yes. We grabbed a few snacks from the vending machine before making the long walk back down the hallway.

As we opened the door to the hospital room, Tommy was delighted to see his grandfather awake. He was smiling in Tommy's direction.

"Hey, boyo, what are you looking so gloomy about?" his grandfather said with a strong but low scratchy voice. "You look sadder than a cheeseburger without any cheese." He coughed and laughed at the same time. "Hey, speaking of cheeseburgers, you should get us both one. I won't tell your dad. It will be our secret."

Tommy smiled wide. He clearly adored his grandfather.

"Now, Mr. Revere, let me get this straight. My grandson says that you let him time-travel, and that you have a talking horse named Liberty who was struck by lightning and transported to modern day, and that you go back in time to visit exceptional Americans like Ben Franklin. Is that right?" Tommy's grandfather asked, with a grin.

"Now that is *supposed* to be a secret," I said, smiling.

"Oh yes, Tommy has quite the imagination," his grandfather said. "But I am impressed with Tommy's new excitement about American history. He told me he actually met Paul Revere and George Washington. Pretty impressive. So I said, let's go back and see some old baseball players like Jackie Robinson and Mel Ott. I have a few questions for those guys."

"That seems like a fantastic idea," I said with a grin. "We will work that into the time-travel schedule."

Tommy's grandfather was alert despite his condition and gave me a wink.

"Listen here, young man," he said to his grandson. "Keep going back in time to find out about our history. American history is wonderful if you pay close attention."

Tommy looked at his grandfather wide-eyed.

"Actually, I tell you what. Look in that drawer over there," his grandfather said.

Tommy walked over to a side table and pulled open the top drawer. He raised his eyebrows in anticipation.

"Is there a notebook in there?" his grandfather asked. "It's not too big, perfect for a shirt pocket."

Tommy pulled out the small flip-top notebook and asked, "This one, Grandpa?"

"Yes, that's it. Why don't you take that notebook on your travels? Write down some great stories to tell me later. I always say if you write it down you have a chance of remembering it," his grandfather said.

"Okay, Grandpa. I'm not the best writer in the world but I will try," Tommy replied. He was standing with straight shoulders.

"I'm sure it will be just fine. Remember to pay attention to the history stuff. I don't really want to read your grocery list," his grandfather joked.

Tommy opened the first page of the notebook and there was a grocery list. He looked at his grandfather and laughed.

Tommy's grandfather was smiling softly now, and while they spoke quietly together, I stepped out into the hallway and met Tommy's dad. He had just returned from the nurses' station.

"I thought I'd give Tommy and his grandpa some alone time," I said.

"Mr. Revere, I cannot tell you how glad I am that you came to visit," Hank said. "As you can see, Tommy's grandfather is very sick. The doctors are trying everything, but he has been undergoing treatment for quite some time."

"Your father seems like a wonderful man and I feel truly honored to be here. Tommy is an amazing student and a super young man. In fact, I was thinking of organizing a field trip for the class. Do you think that would help Tommy take his mind off of things for a little while?"

"I think that sounds like a perfect idea, Mr. Revere," Hank replied. "This has been a difficult time for him. Tommy should be around his friends, or the Crew as he calls them, and just have fun."

We returned to the room and I spent a few minutes telling Tommy about the field trip idea. His grandfather had fallen asleep again and was resting peacefully.

"See you soon, Tommy," I said. "I will text you after speaking with Freedom's and Cam's parents and receiving permission from Principal Sherman."

Tommy smiled and nodded, and I shook Hank's hand as I left.

As I exited the hospital, the rain cleared and I found Liberty waiting where I left him. Surprisingly, he seemed to have avoided trouble this time.

I patted the side of his neck and said, "Liberty, I'm glad you're here. How are the ants in your pants?"

Liberty said, "Wait, what do you mean? I don't have any ants in my pants."

"Oh, really? Because Tommy and I saw you practicing your dance moves from the window and it looked like you had ants in your pants."

Liberty rolled his eyes. "Ants in my pants? That's the best rhyme you've got? Ha! While you guys were all snug as a bug in a rug, I was pretty smug, cutting the rug, and doing the jitterbug. It was a game, escaping the rain."

"And since when did this turn into a rhyming competition?" I replied.

"Just now, that's how. And we need to meet on where to get something to eat!"

I stared at Liberty in wonder. Where does he come up with this stuff? I smiled and said, "Well, right now, we have to start on our plan."

"Um, plan? Like planning for a picnic with lots of food? Or for a day at the spa? Or maybe for an all-you-can-eat . . ."

I could hear Liberty's stomach growling.

"Don't worry, I brought you a snack from the cafeteria," I said, giving him an apple.

"One apple, that's it? You were in there *forever*," Liberty said sulking, then added, "Oh, sorry I was just thinking of myself. How is Tommy? Oh, I hope he is okay. Did he get anything to eat because it would be really nice if he had a good snack like pudding, or cake, or ice cream, or donuts or—"

I interrupted Liberty's seemingly endless commentary and said, "Actually, I was talking about planning a field trip. I really think Tommy needs some time with his friends. Since I'm not teaching a class this semester, I thought we could take the Crew on a special field trip during fall break."

Liberty's eyes lit up and he said, "Oh, a field trip, I'm totally in! The field part reminds me of a pasture, which reminds me of hay, which reminds me of lunch, which reminds me we haven't had lunch. And I'm pretty sure an apple is not going to do it."

"You are right," I chuckled. "Let's go put some fuel in that tank of yours."

It didn't take long for Principal Sherman to agree to the idea. He said he was impressed with how much history the students were learning, and thought it would be a good experience for them. We just needed to get signed permission slips from the Crew's parents, and we would be off. I had a train trip in mind, and then an adventure through the time portal to American history.

Chapter 2

The next morning I spoke with Tommy's, Freedom's, and Cam's parents and they all thought the trip was a great idea. In fact, Freedom's grandfather offered to come along as a chaperone. By the end of the week we were on our way to the Main Street train station.

Once there, we all carried our packs onto the platform. After a few minutes, a whistle blew and a large train rumbled into the station. Car after car rolled past with the sound of whining brakes and the smell of diesel fuel. When the train came to a complete stop, a voice from the overhead speakers said, "Now boarding all passengers departing to Washington, D.C., the nation's capital. Please board on Track One."

I took a deep breath and looked around to make sure I had not lost anyone. Silently, I checked off their names in my head: Tommy, Cam, Freedom, and Freedom's grandfather. Collectively, they were known as the Time-Traveling

Crew, because they all had time-traveled before. Well, with the exception of Freedom's grandfather.

"I sure hope Liberty gets on the train," Tommy said, as he swung his backpack over his shoulder.

Freedom whispered, "Liberty turned invisible and is heading for the baggage car. But he's not happy about it. He thinks he should be traveling in coach with us." I admired Freedom's special relationship with Liberty. She amazingly could speak with him using only her mind, and they were very close friends. When we met George Washington, she even braided Liberty's mane.

"I'm pretty sure they don't allow horses in the passenger cars," Cam said, as he flicked a yo-yo up and down like a pro. "Maybe they could strap Liberty to the top? Could you imagine?" Cam laughed.

"Yeah, but he'd probably get bugs up his nose," Tommy said, smiling.

"Don't worry about Liberty," I said. "I included an extra pouch with twenty pounds of oats for him to eat. I doubt he'll even miss us."

We lifted our backpacks and boarded the train.

The conductor closed the door behind us and we were off on our new adventure.

"Washington, D.C., here we come!" I exclaimed, as we walked up the stairs. Before we were seated, the train started moving and rocking back and forth. Cam and Tommy bumped each other as we walked down the narrow aisle to our seats. They were pretending the bumps were unintentional.

"Here we are," I said. "Try to put your bags under your seats or in the cabin above."

"I'm pretty sure I need a ladder to get up there, Mr. Revere," Cam said with a smirk.

"Good point," I said, laughing. "Let me help you."

The train was moving out of the station.

Out of the blue, Tommy said, "Remember when we time-traveled to 1775 and chased after Paul Revere trying to avoid being caught by British spies? That was crazy."

"Sure do. What made you think of that?" I asked, as I placed another bag in the overhead compartment.

"Look over there. That conductor guy is lurking in the aisle like a spy," Tommy said, grinning.

It was really good to see Tommy joking again. As I put Tommy's bag overhead, his football fell out and rolled on the floor.

Freedom's grandfather picked up the ball and threw a short toss to Tommy, who grabbed it with both hands and made a running motion. The narrow aisle forced him to knock into a seat or two.

"My grandpa throws it just like that," Tommy said, looking up at Freedom's grandfather.

"Well, your grandpa must have a good arm like me," Freedom's grandfather said. "I was a quarterback in high school. Really loved it. And boy, did the girls think I was cute, especially Freedom's grandma." He chuckled loudly as Tommy tossed the ball back.

Freedom blushed. "Grandpa!" she exclaimed.

"Well, it's true, Freedom, I was quite a catch back then," Freedom's grandfather said. He was teasing her, so she just shook her head happily and took out her drawing pad.

Freedom's grandfather wore a tweed coat and hat. His hair

and eyes were dark like Freedom's, with a kind face and very few wrinkles for a man his age. He smiled and held my shoulder as we took our seats, and said, "Thank you for this wonderful opportunity to spend time with my granddaughter."

"Actually, you're doing me a favor," I replied. "It is really nice to have another adult along. Traveling with these guys is like herding cats." I chuckled, thinking especially of the really *large* cat that couldn't ride with us. I hoped Liberty was behaving himself. I took off my tricorner hat and placed it on my lap.

"Grandpa," Freedom said, nudging his arm. He had a slight stoop to his strong shoulders, "Mr. Revere is an amazing substitute teacher. He took us to meet Americans in history like William Bradford and Squanto during the first Thanksgiving," she said.

"That is superb," Freedom's grandfather replied smiling. "You mean you met them in a museum, right?"

"No, no, we met them in person back in 1621," Freedom explained.

Freedom's grandfather looked a little confused but raised his eyebrows and nodded. "Oh, okay," he said.

Cam added, "Yeah, and we met the guy who invented swim fins and bifocal glasses!"

"Oh yeah, ol' Benjamin Franklin was legit," Tommy said.

"I think I like George Washington the most, though," Cam said, "One day I want to talk to him more about other strategies to win at dodgeball. I mean, he led the American underdogs to win the war."

"Yeah, and then Cam led the Eagle underdogs to a victory over Billy the Bully," Tommy remembered, giving him a high five.

Freedom's grandfather winked at me as if I were the best teacher in the world. Little did he know, we really *did* meet these amazing Americans in person during our time travels back in history. Sometimes even I could not believe the amazing places we had seen with our magical friend Liberty. It is incredible that we already visited the Pilgrims and Native Americans at the first Thanksgiving, Samuel Adams and the American Patriots at the Boston Tea Party, and Dr. Joseph Warren at the Battle of Bunker Hill. We've nearly fallen overboard on the high seas, fought with swords, and made forts.

"Well, it's obvious you've learned a lot," Freedom's grandpa remarked.

I said, "Hey, how about we head to the café car? We can plan out the details of our trip while we have a snack."

"Now we're talking," said Cam. "I'm starving."

"That sounds like something Liberty would say," Tommy teased. He seemed to be cheering up a bit but still wasn't his usual self.

We walked toward the next car, and the Crew jumped one by one over the space between the railcars.

"Cam, why don't you lead the group and look for a sign that says café?" I said. "And don't get into any trouble."

I stood back to wait for Freedom's grandfather and saw Tommy playfully bump into Freedom as they both knocked into a seat cushion. Before Freedom could retaliate, a man in a neighboring seat abruptly woke up from his nap and glanced at them.

"Sorry," Freedom said. "My friend is clumsy. He walks like a duck."

Tommy replied, "Quack, quack," and quickly pulled Freedom to her feet and they both hurried past.

As the Crew ran ahead I had a minute to speak with Freedom's grandfather. I said, "Tommy is having some trouble right now, in case he looks a little down. His grandfather is ill and in the hospital. They are very close."

"Oh, I am so sorry to hear that," Freedom's grandfather said, his eyes full of emotion. "Freedom and I have a special relationship, and I certainly understand how difficult that must be for Tommy. My wife was ill for a long time, and Freedom had a very tough time."

"Yes, it is awful, but I hope this trip with his friends will cheer him up and be a wonderful learning experience," I said.

"That sounds perfect. I will be here to help in any way I can. And I am really excited about the trip," Freedom's grandfather said with a kind smile.

By the time we reached the café car, the Crew had already grabbed two tables near large windows. We sat down and I admired the brown and yellow leaves passing in a blur. It was a joy to look out the window at several towns and states on the way to our nation's capital.

"What's for breakfast?" Cam asked, pulling out a yo-yo and placing it on the table.

"You gotta teach me some of your yo-yo tricks," Tommy said. "I brought my football, too, in case we have time to play in Washington, D.C. Oh, and I brought some snacks. You know, in case we're bored and hungry."

Freedom added, "I brought my charcoal pencils and a few books to read if we have any time in the hotel."

"Oh, do you think there is any room service?" Cam asked. "I want to have a hamburger brought up to the room and we can watch TV. There is this really cool show—"

"There will be so many cool things to learn about in Washington, D.C., you won't have time for TV," I interjected.

"There is always time for TV, Mr. Revere," Cam said with a grin. He started to flick his yo-yo but I shook my head.

"What does everyone want to eat?" I asked and took all orders. After a few minutes I brought back a variety of snacks.

After everyone took their first bite I said, "Who wants to play trivia? You know I can't go for long without a little history trivia."

"Are there prizes?" Cam asked looking up from his sandwich.

"As a matter of fact there is for the winner," I said in a joking tone, winking at Cam. "But I thought you just liked to play for history bragging rights. Just kidding. The person who gets the most questions correct gets a twenty-five-dollar gift card from a store of your choice."

"I'm in!" Tommy shouted.

"Me, too," Freedom said.

Cam followed with "All right, me three."

"Can anyone tell me to what place in history we last time-traveled?" I asked.

Freedom's grandfather looked at me with a slight grin. I'm sure he thought all of this time-travel talk was part of my teaching strategy.

"Totally easy," Cam said raising his hand, "We went to see the Declaration of Independence. The date was July 4, 1776, to be exact."

"Correct. Well done, Cam; point to you."

"Since that was an easy one, can anyone tell me why the American colonists were declaring independence and from what country?" I asked.

"I got this!" Tommy shouted as if he were catching a baseball in the outfield. "The Americans wanted to be free from the King of England. They wanted to have their own country without all of the pointless rules."

"Whoa, what geniuses you are. Point to you Tommy," I said, entirely thrilled.

"Also, the Americans wanted to have their own land and believe in God without being stopped," Freedom added.

"You are correct too, Freedom. Point to you," I replied enthusiastically.

Freedom's grandpa lovingly tapped her on the shoulder and said, "Great job, Freedom."

"You each have a point. For a tiebreaker . . . let's see . . . I wonder what a tricky one could be. Okay, got it. Does anyone know how long it took the Americans to *actually* become free and really independent? Meaning, how long did the war go on from the time the Americans first declared independence in 1776 to when they were actually independent?"

"I think it was like six more years," Tommy said uncertainly.

"Wow! Very close, Tommy," I said. "General Washington and the Continental Army actually had to fight for another *seven* years. But I am going to give you a point because you were very close, and it is difficult to remember exact years. The key is to know it was a long, drawn-out war and very difficult. But General Washington and the Patriots persevered and won. He was a true hero."

Freedom's grandfather was smiling.

I said, "So you all know that the Americans declared independence from Great Britain in 1776, and won *actual* independence in 1783. Now does anyone know who the capital city is named after?"

"George Washington!" they all shouted, including Freedom's grandpa, caught up in the moment.

"That was too easy, Mr. Revere," Cam said.

"Well, I guess you guys are just too smart. Tommy wins this round of trivia. When we get to Washington you can pick out your gift card," I said.

Tommy took a bow.

Seizing the moment, I added, "Here's a few more factoids for you. Washington, D.C., was established in the U.S. Constitution as the nation's capital. Washington's current location was based on a deal struck by the northern and southern states. George Washington chose the site and the city was founded on July 16, 1790."

All of a sudden Freedom started looking around. She shook her head, tapping me on the arm and pointing. Out of nowhere two one-dollar bills appeared on the café restaurant bar, and a piece of bread flew on its own through the air.

"Liberty," I said with a serious whisper, "get over here, and stay camouflaged in case someone sees you."

The piece of bread dropped to the floor as if someone had just turned off the antigravity switch.

All of a sudden I remembered that Freedom's grandfather did not know about Liberty's special abilities. My stomach sank, but I knew I had to come clean.

I turned to Freedom's grandfather and said, "There is something that you should know. You are part of the Crew now, and because of that I am going to tell you a secret and hope you'll keep it confidential. Since you'll be spending quite a bit of time with us you should know Liberty can talk and he has the uncanny ability to perfectly camouflage into his surroundings."

Liberty exhaled and suddenly appeared in the train carriage.

All eyes turned to Liberty while I scanned to make sure no one else was in the café car.

Freedom's grandfather stared at me and then at Liberty. It felt like everyone was holding their breath anticipating what I would say next.

"Yes, I know it sounds strange and, frankly, impossible," I said. "But it's true. Liberty, what would you like to say?"

Liberty replied, "Were you trying to do the game without me, Revere?" He was giving me the eye.

"Of course not, Liberty. I was just warming up the crowd with history trivia. I knew you would want to make a grand entrance. I just didn't think it would be here and now."

"Well, lucky for you, I have arrived," Liberty said with a dramatic bow.

Freedom's grandfather looked at Liberty, then at the kids, and then back at Liberty. He was shaking his head, eyes wide.

"So, Liberty, since you delightfully decided to join us, why don't you help explain the game," I said. "But do it quick. I'm still not sure how I'm going to explain a horse in the café car."

"Why, I thought you would never ask!" Liberty exclaimed.

He cleared his throat and started in a low dramatic voice: "This is your mission, if you choose to accept it. I am your commander. I need to know everything there is to know about our nation's capital. You are my special agents. Captain Revere, please show the orders for MISSION: WASHINGTON, D.C., and pass them to the agents."

Following the commander's lead I held up the printed five-by-seven cards for everyone to see.

Liberty continued, "Here are your orders, special agents. The code word is MILKSHAKE."

MISSION: WASHINGTON D.C.

TOP SECRET

This is your mission,
if you choose to accept it.

CODE NAME:
MILKSHAKE

1 POINT PER TASK

OBJECTIVES:

1. **UNION STATION** – Take photo in the middle of Union Station. One point to first Secret Agent to send photo to Rush Revere/Liberty.

2. **WASHINGTON MONUMENT** – One point to first Secret Agent to give the correct answer to Commander Liberty's clue to Rush Revere/Liberty.

3. **NATIONAL ARCHIVES** – One point to first Secret Agent to give the correct answer to Commander Liberty's clue to Rush Revere/Liberty.

4. **U.S. CAPITOL BUILDING** – One point to first Secret Agent to give the correct answer to Commander Liberty's clue to Rush Revere/Liberty.

5. **SUPREME COURT OF THE UNITED STATES** – One point to first Secret Agent to give the correct answer to Commander Liberty's clue to Rush Revere/Liberty.

6. **WHITE HOUSE** – Two points to the first Secret Agent to give the correct answer to Commander Liberty's clue to Rush Revere/Liberty.

DOUBLE POINTS
2 Points for the Task

Good Luck,
Liberty

Adventures of
RUSH REVERE

Cam looked at Freedom and Tommy and said, "Milkshake?" They all giggled.

Liberty didn't skip a beat and said, "The agent who gathers the most information on this card will gain the rank of Super Scout! And, for the record, you get double points for the last objective. So I would highly suggest paying attention to that section of your card."

"Does the Super Scout get a prize?" Tommy asked, feeling confident from his trivia win.

"Why yes indeed, but the prize is top secret," Liberty replied, nodding with a serious look as if he knew confidential information.

Everyone looked at him waiting for further information, but clearly for dramatic effect Liberty said nothing.

"Who can tell me the first task on this mission?" I asked, looking down at the objectives on the card.

Freedom carefully read the top lines following each word with her finger. "Got it, Captain! We need to take a picture in the middle of Union Station."

"Correct," Liberty replied, continuing his deep voice. "The first agent to text Captain Revere the photo gets the point!"

Freedom's grandfather leaned in and said to Liberty, "This will be great fun. I can help with the clues if you need an extra hand or hoof."

Over the loudspeaker a voice said, "Now arriving at Union Station, Washington, D.C. Please remain seated until the train comes to a complete stop."

The train hummed into the station and Liberty took a deep breath and disappeared. Soon the car doors were open and we exited in single file, then walked across the platform and through a massive hall.

Cam pointed and shouted, "Look, that's gotta be the center of the station! I'm gonna take a picture for Liberty!"

"Nice work, just be sure to stay where I can see you," I warned, as Cam darted off.

Freedom and Tommy raced after him, phones in hand. I heard three beeps one after the other on my phone. Eventually, Freedom's grandfather and I caught up and we all headed for the exit. As we made our way through the doors, we were welcomed by the crisp autumn air to Washington, D.C. Commuters rushed to and fro, along with cars, buses, and taxis.

"Mr. Revere, look at the American flags!" Tommy said, pointing up.

Sure enough, there were three large American flags flying on three different flagpoles. Each had a bronze golden eagle sitting on top, welcoming visitors to the nation's capital.

"Quick—pop quiz," I said. "Does anyone know how the bald eagle became a symbol of our country?"

"Because it is strong and serious?" Liberty answered.

"Oh, very good answer, Liberty," I replied. "You are both smart and talented."

Liberty puffed out his chest and stood tall.

"The eagle has long been a symbol of strength and freedom in the United States. As a matter of fact, the bald eagle was chosen way back on June 20, 1772, when the Continental Congress created the Great Seal of the United States. Secretary of Congress Charles Thomson made the eagle prominent and it remains so today," I said.

"I love eagles, Mr. Revere," Freedom said. "I mean, I haven't actually seen one in person but I have lots of pictures of eagles flying. They are beautiful."

"They sure are, and very rare. You would be lucky to see a bald eagle in the wild," I replied.

"Speaking of flying, this may be kind of a dumb question, but those flags made me think of it," Tommy said. "Why is our flag red, white, and blue?"

"That isn't a dumb question at all, Tommy. In fact, it is a great question," I replied.

"When the Great Seal was chosen, there was no specific meaning for the red, white, and blue. So Secretary Thomson said that white signifies purity and innocence; red, hardiness and valor; and blue, vigilance, perseverance, and justice."

"Oh that's totally cool. Oh wait, this is a good one for Grandpa's notebook," Tommy said, pulling out his pencil.

"If you really want to impress him, you should also say the first American flag had only thirteen stars representing the thirteen states and now has fifty representing the fifty states," I said.

"Nice. I'll totally add that," Tommy replied.

Suddenly, Liberty appeared behind us and nuzzled the back of my neck.

"I can see you have a special relationship with your horse," said Freedom's grandpa.

"Yes," I replied. "He's one of a kind."

All right, everyone," I announced. "I assume you all have your backpacks, phones, games, yo-yos, and whatever else you brought with you?"

Everyone nodded.

"Good, then follow me. Our hotel is not too far from here," I said.

Cam, Freedom, and Tommy seemed giddy with excitement.

Cam and Tommy were laughing and high-fiving every few feet. Freedom was quietly absorbing everything around her.

So far the plan to distract Tommy from all he had been dealing with was working. He was starting to look like a playful kid again.

Freedom's grandfather seemed to pay close attention to the buildings, signs, and commuters as we walked. He said, "There is a unique energy in this city. We are at the political heart of the country."

After fifteen minutes we arrived at our hotel and checked in. I helped Liberty find a quiet sheltered park and gave him enough to eat for the night. He was not pleased but accepted the arrangements. Once everyone was settled, I found a seat in the lobby, took out my map, and finalized the plan for the next day.

The next morning we would take our first ride on the underground subway train, called the Metro. I couldn't wait to take the Crew to the first stop on our tour of Washington, D.C.

Also, I had a time-travel adventure planned that they would not soon forget.

Chapter 3

*H*ave you been on a subway before?" I asked the group, as we went down an escalator to the underground station in the early morning.

"I have once, in Boston," Freedom said. She held on to the edge of the escalator as we went down. "But I don't like the really tall escalators they have here."

Freedom's grandfather put his hand on her shoulder and said in a calm voice, "Here in Washington they call the subway the Metro. They are trains that go underground. It is a great way to avoid traffic in the city. All we have to do is get down this long escalator and we are off on our adventure."

At the bottom, Freedom jumped off the escalator as quickly as she could. We made our way to the edge of the platform and through the sliding doors to the subway car. People entered and exited, some dressed in suits, others in baseball caps and jeans.

"People-watching is one of the best parts of visiting a new city," I said, holding on to a rail above me as the Metro car moved through the dark tunnel.

"I am pretty sure there are a lot of people watching *you*, Mr. Revere," Cam said smiling, trying to keep his feet steady on the floor. Of course, he was referring to my colonial-era clothing.

"What can I say? They know a good-looking hat when they see one," I said. An older woman looked at me sideways as she pretended to read a book.

"Keep holding on tight. We should be there in a minute or two," I said. "Our first visit in Washington will be to the Washington Monument, then the National Archives, home to our most important documents."

"Liberty says he's going to try to beat us on foot," Freedom said.

"He might," I said. "It's really not that far, especially for a horse."

A voice from the overhead speaker announced, "Next stop, Federal Triangle station."

"That's us, right, Mr. Revere?" asked Tommy. I noticed he had taken his football out of his backpack and was tossing it up and down with one hand.

After another nervous escalator ride for Freedom, we came out of underground darkness into bright daylight. All around us were trees and green fields, framed by a blue sky.

We gathered together off to the side to get out of the way of hustling commuters.

"Where are we going first?" Tommy asked.

I pulled out my map of Washington, D.C., and said, "The National Mall."

White House

Pennsylvania Avenue

Washington Monument

Constitution Avenue

Lincoln Memorial

Independence Avenue

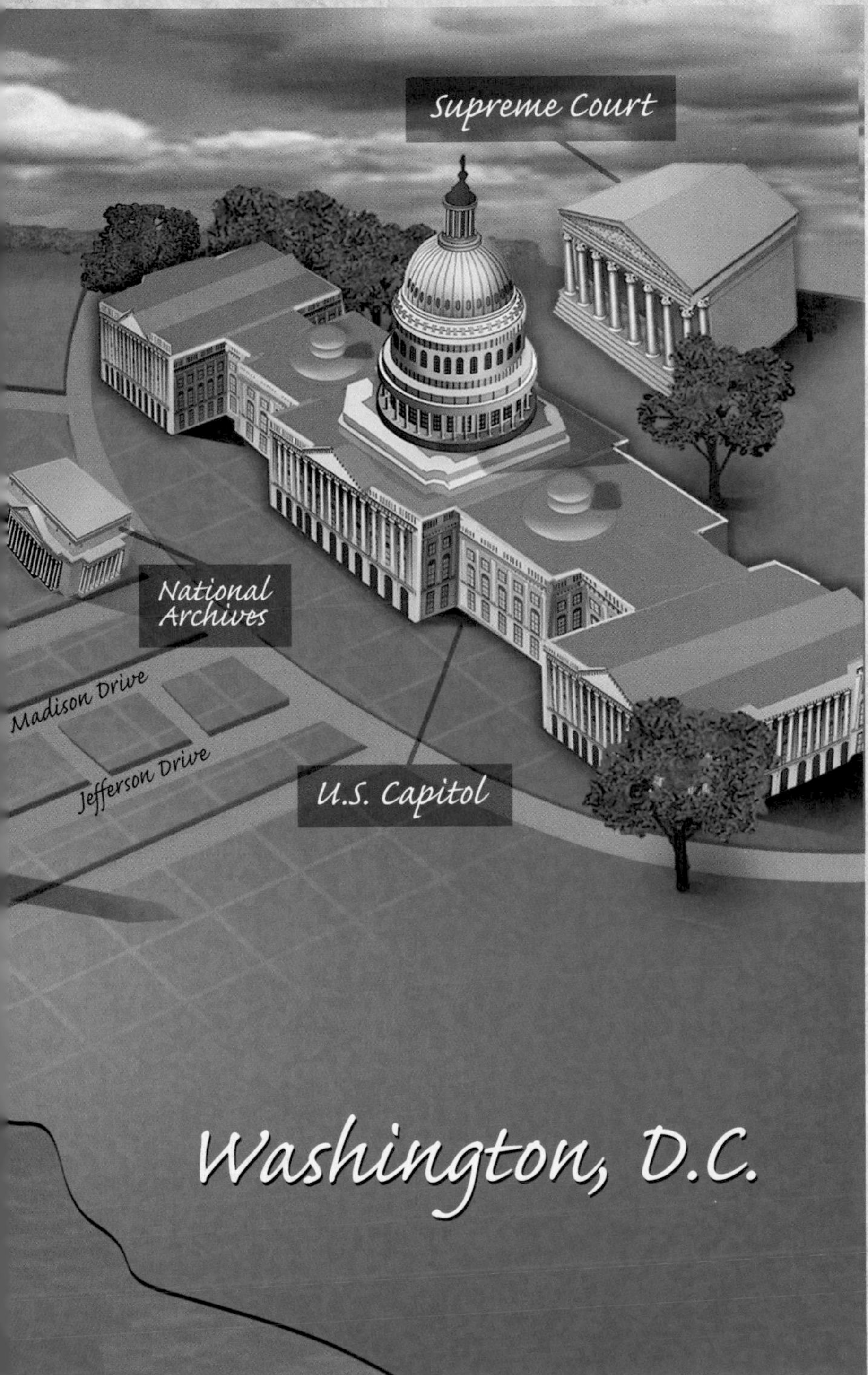

Supreme Court

National
Archives

Madison Drive

Jefferson Drive

U.S. Capitol

Washington, D.C.

"Sweet!" Cam exclaimed, "Let's go to the food court for a jumbo hot dog."

"Shopping spree!" Tommy joined in. It was nice to see him joking again.

"Very funny, guys. We are not going to a mall with stores like Macy's or a food court," I replied.

Freedom and her grandfather both laughed.

"The National Mall is the long, famous stretch from the U.S. Capitol Building to the Lincoln Memorial," I said.

Freedom's grandfather added, "The National Mall is known around the world for housing our iconic national monuments."

We walked for a few blocks.

"Wow, Mr. Revere, there's the Washington Monument!" said Cam, pointing over my shoulder.

"Hey, that's cool," Tommy said. "My grandpa sent me a postcard once with the Washington Monument on it. He says you can recognize the tall white structure anywhere and know it is our nation's capital."

"Quick, another pop quiz," I said. "Who can tell me how many American flags surround the base of the monument?"

The crew surveyed the scene and I knew they were quickly counting flags in their heads. Knowing how good Tommy is with math, I expected him to answer first. However, it was Freedom who muttered softly and uncertainly, "Fifty flags?"

"Wow, you were fast, Freedom. Good job," said Tommy.

"Excellent, Freedom. You are right," I replied. "The fifty flags represent our fifty states. And the Washington Monument was one of the first attractions in Washington, D.C., and was built in tribute to the first president, Cam's friend George Washington."

"Can we go up the Washington Monument like the Empire State Building? That would be way cool," Cam said.

"You can, but there are a lot of stairs. We may be tired before we even start," I joked.

We decided to walk toward the monument so that the Crew could get a better look. In Washington, D.C., the city blocks are wide and long, and the walk was good exercise. Tommy threw his football to Freedom and Cam as we walked. When we arrived, we all stood at the base looking up at its height.

"Since Liberty is not here right now, he asked me to give you the next clue on your mission," Freedom's grandfather said. He glanced down as his Mission: Washington, D.C., card.

"Liberty is grabbing a snack and will meet us at the National Archives," I added.

Freedom's grandfather continued: "The first to text the correct answer to Mr. Revere wins the point. Your clue is:

> How many steps does the Washington Monument have, and how tall is it?

All of a sudden Tommy ran toward a sign with details about the Washington Monument.

"Got it!" he said, pumping his fist in the air.

"The Washington Monument has 897 steps and is over 555 feet high," Tommy said out loud, forgetting he wasn't supposed to tell the other secret agents. Then he started typing into his phone. Cam and Freedom quickly began typing, too, and my phone beeped three times.

"It looks like Tommy got that one first," I said. "Well done!"

"Good job, Tommy!" Freedom's grandfather exclaimed.

This is a view of the Washington Monument in Washington, D.C.
Do you see the reflection in the Reflecting Pool?

As I looked at the Washington Monument I was reminded of my family. "I once toured the monument with my brother when we were kids and we walked down all of those stairs. I remember every single step. It was a workout. We were huffing and puffing," I said.

"Oh man, I'm tired just thinking about it," Tommy responded. "But that's really awesome. I bet you can see really far from up there. Does it have a cool lookout like a fort?"

"As a matter of fact, yes, it does. You can see thirty miles or more of the city," I said.

After a few seconds of discussion, we all decided not to climb the Washington Monument this time. The walk to the National Archives would make us tired enough, and we still had lots to do.

We set off walking and after about twenty minutes arrived near the National Archives, Freedom pointed and said, "Look, there's Liberty across the street."

"Hey, Liberty!" Tommy called out, waving his arm. "It looks like he's waiting for us in front of that building."

Liberty stood beside a flagpole with the American flag waving above. Tourists sat on the steps beside him. The Crew obeyed the traffic signals, then ran over to him.

"Why, fancy meeting you here," Liberty said, in an English accent, for some reason.

The kids smiled and hugged him with genuine affection. Even Freedom's grandpa rubbed Liberty's nose.

The giant stone building was breathtaking. It looked like something out of Greek mythology. There were steps that resembled marble, leading from the road up to the main entrance. A row of stark white stone pillars stood like guardians in front.

Tommy read the words carved in stone out loud: "'Archives of the United States of America.' Hey, that must be the National Archives, right, Mr. Revere?"

Cam smirked at Tommy and said, "What gave you that idea?"

Tommy punched him in the arm.

"Are you special agents ready for your next clue?" Liberty asked. He looked to be preparing for a long speech.

"Hold on one second, Liberty, before you start the clue. Let me tell you guys about the National Archives. Do you see those words?" I said, pointing to a massive stone statue of a mother and child in front of the building.

THE HERITAGE OF THE PAST
IS THE SEED THAT BRINGS FORTH
THE HARVEST OF THE FUTURE

"Does anyone know what these words mean?"

"I know, I know," Liberty said, raising a hoof. "It means that if you plant apple seeds, you can harvest the apples and eat lots of juicy fruit."

"Very close, Liberty," I said. "It basically means that when you plant a seed it will eventually grow to become a tree. If you create something in the present day, it will become something good or bad in the future. It is therefore important to know and protect our history."

Freedom raised her hand. "I really like the statue. It is really beautiful. Could we all take a picture in front of it?"

"Of course!" I said. "Now one last thing before the clue. Much like a library, the National Archives keeps important documents both from history and from today. That is why it is so big."

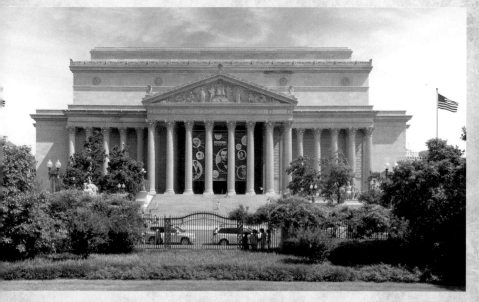

Do you know what famous American documents
are kept here at the National Archives?

"Come on, Captain! Can I continue the mission now?" Liberty asked, with a frustrated tone. Then, realizing he was the center of attention, he stood up straight and cleared his voice, as if he were about to speak to thousands of people.

The kids all chuckled.

"On second thought, before you do, I have to tell everybody what we are going to see inside the National Archives building," I said, annoying Liberty again.

Liberty made a gesture of pure exasperation but I pushed on. "Inside there are three of the most important documents in our country's history—the Declaration of Independence, the Constitution, and the Bill of Rights. The actual documents, created hundreds of years ago, are right through that door."

"That's really cool, Mr. Revere. There is a poster of the Declaration of Independence on our wall at school. I just thought it was a poster. I didn't know there was a real one somewhere," Cam said.

"Okay, okay, now that we know what's in the National Archives, let's get back to the mission, pleaaaaaasssssseee. Are you ready? Steady? Super ready steady?" Liberty said.

I looked over at Liberty with a sideward eye roll, encouraging him to move his dramatic delivery along. I was ready to run through the entrance, giddy with anticipation.

Liberty continued, "Okay, special agents. You need to find the answer to this clue somewhere inside the building and report back to me at base camp with the answer. It must be written down."

I helped pull a note written by Liberty out of his saddlebag. It read:

I can be found in a special painting on the wall of the National Archives. I have a leg with a peg and stand behind a sword. What is my name and where did you find me?

All three kids looked a little confused, while Freedom's grand-father smiled as if he knew something we did not.

Liberty looked serious, like a game show host in the final round, and said, "I will wait out here and if you bring back the correct answer you will get a point. Good luck."

After a pause he added, "While you are searching, if you happen to find a nice cool glass of spinach smoothie, feel free to bring that back, too. Just sayin'."

"Try not to get into any trouble for a change," I said.

"I am deeply offended. That hurts me to the core. Now, what would make you think little old me would get into any kind of trouble? Gosh," Liberty replied.

I just shook my head.

We entered the National Archives through a side door. We passed the metal detectors like an airport and were in. On the wall a sign said NO PHOTOGRAPHY ALLOWED.

Cam pulled out his yo-yo and started doing tricks until Freedom's grandfather motioned for him to pay attention.

Near a wall, I noticed a portable bookstand full of maps. We stopped and studied the map for a minute, and determined that an elevator ride up was the quickest way to the documents.

"Rotunda?" Cam asked as we entered the elevator. "That kinda sounds like 'Rot, Undar' in an Australian accent. I don't know about you, but I don't think I'd like to visit anything that rots," Cam said with a smirk.

"Ha, me either," Tommy said. Freedom's grandfather shook his head with a half smile.

"Well, lucky for you, the Rotunda does not rot. It's actually pronounced 'Ro,' like 'Row Your Boat.' In ancient Greece, they called the type of room that we are about to visit a rotunda, because of the curved walls and dome."

When the elevator doors opened, the first thing I noticed was the floors. They were spotless. Everything looked pristine, like an old-fashioned bank vault. There was a chill of cool air.

"Look up ahead, there's the Rotunda," Freedom's grandfather said, picking up his pace. He motioned for the kids to hurry behind. It was funny to see Tommy, Freedom, and Cam uniformly follow behind like a mother duck and her ducklings.

I caught up in time to say, "Take a minute to really absorb this. The room you are about to enter is called the Rotunda for the Charters of Freedom. The three precious documents—the Declaration of Independence, the Constitution, and the Bill of Rights—are right here."

Tommy looked at Freedom and whispered, "How does it feel to be named after something so important? Maybe we should be carrying you on our shoulders."

She gave Tommy a shove and softly laughed, saying, "The next thing you'll want to do is put me under museum glass."

Tommy raised his eyebrows. "Hey, not a bad idea."

Freedom pushed him again and rolled her eyes. Cam pulled out his yo-yo again, and quickly put it back as a guard looked at him.

In front of us there were huge open gates that looked like the entrance to the Emerald City in *The Wizard of Oz*. On each side and on the far end, American flags stood tall around the documents.

Do you know what important document this is?
It is the Constitution of the United States, and it is more
than two hundred years old. It remains the law of the land today.

Have you heard of the freedom of speech? It is contained in the Bill of Rights, which are the first ten Amendments or changes to the U.S. Constitution. As George Mason said, it protects the rights of the people.

Tommy said, smiling, "Don't forget we have to find a painting with a peg leg and a sword. You know, the usual."

Cam laughed and said, "True, we're on it."

We walked through the gates and into the dome. The lighting was soft and dim with spotlights focused on the glass cases, like a fine art museum.

"Hey, look, it's the Declaration of Independence," Cam said.

"Where, where, I want to see," Freedom said, getting closer to Cam as we looked into the case.

The ink was faded and the paper was brown but the document looked like the most valuable diamond in a jewelry case.

"I wish I could write like that," Freedom said, leaning in to look closely at the beautiful script. In some places on the old parchment the handwriting had almost turned invisible.

At the top were the words *In Congress July 4, 1776,* in large print.

"Mr. Revere, we were actually there!" Cam said excitedly. "Look, you can see the signatures of our friends from the Second Continental Congress. I think that is Ben Franklin and John Hancock. Remember we saw him in Lexington with grumpy old Samuel Adams?"

"Of course I do," I said, still amazed at our time travels.

A soft light lit up the page. The paper was almost poster-sized and looked as fragile as silk. The script had faded into the brown page, and the bottom was creased with dark spots.

"That is the *actual* Declaration of Independence," Freedom's grandfather said. "That piece of paper is hundreds of years old."

"Yes, this is the very document the Patriots created to declare independence from Great Britain," I whispered. "They fought the Revolutionary War to end the abuses of the British king. You see the famous words here—*all men are created equal.* The King did not believe this simple statement."

"Hey, guys, look up," Tommy said, pointing. "There's a painting, like in Liberty's clue."

A huge painting covered the wall above us, with a plaque that read:

> *We hold these truths to be self evident,*
> *that all men are created equal . . .*

"Wow, that looks as big as a football field," Cam said, as we all looked up.

Freedom's grandfather pointed to a sign indicating that this painting was called *The Declaration,* by Barry Faulkner.

"Look for the guy with the peg leg," Tommy said.

Freedom took out her sketchpad and drew the scene.

"Hey, wait a minute," Cam said. "I know that guy. Look at the dude in yellow, the third guy from the left. That's our friend Ben Franklin. Oh, and there's Thomas Jefferson."

"Yes, you're exactly right! It looks just like it did on our visit in 1776," I said, realizing the people around us might think I was nutty.

"Shoot, no peg leg. Where is that guy?" Tommy asked.

"Gather round, guys and gals," I said. "If you look carefully, you will notice everyone who was involved in writing the Declaration of Independence is there in the mural. Do you recognize anyone else?"

"I do," Freedom said, raising her hand. "Samuel Adams."

"Spot-on. Brilliant, Freedom!" I said.

I could have stayed there all day, but other tourists wanted their chance.

Freedom's grandfather led us to the next case. "Who can tell me what this document is?" he asked.

The kids got close and looked down. For some reason, Cam had his yo-yo back in his hand again. So I asked him to put it away.

"I know, it is the Constitution," Tommy said.

"Correct," Freedom's grandfather replied.

"What gave it away? The sign that says U.S. Constitution?" Cam joked, giving Tommy a small jab in the arm.

"Actually, no, I know a constitution when I see one," Tommy jabbed back.

I explained: "The United States Constitution is our country's most important document. At the time it was written, the words were radical."

Freedom's grandfather added, "Yes, it is a physical document, but it is a foundation that established an entirely new way of governing. The power under the Constitution remains always with the people. Just like when you build a house, you have to start with a solid foundation. That way the house will stay strong and not crumble."

"That is really pretty cool," Cam said. "But look how short it is. How can it cover everything? I mean there are lots of people and different laws, right?"

"That is the amazing part," I added. "This document, created by our friends like George Washington, established the incredible system of government we know today. Have you heard of the balance of power, checks and balances, the President, elected Congress, and the Supreme Court?"

The kids nodded cautiously.

"Well, those things *never* existed in human history, until our ancestors, the Founders, created them in the Constitution. And here it is, the actual document itself."

The kids looked down at the case, studying the paper, ink, and words carefully.

Freedom's grandfather asked, "Wouldn't you just love to ask the Founders how they came up with all this stuff out of the blue? I sure would."

Freedom said, "They must have been really smart."

"Very true," I said. "There was one man in particular who was brilliant. His name is James Madison, and he is known as the 'Father of the Constitution.' He studied really hard and worked with others to come up with the framework for government, seen here in the Constitution."

"So what does the Constitution *do?*" Cam asked.

"What do you mean, Cam?" I replied, confused.

"Well, it is a document from hundreds of years ago but I am not sure what it does exactly."

"I see. The Constitution is a set of laws that govern the country. It ensures that the people have rights using a system including a president, Congress, and Supreme Court. We will learn more about all of these, but the thing to remember is that the Constitution sets the laws for the country to protect the people of the United States," I said.

Tommy said, "Got it. I share a bedroom with my older brother. Our bedroom was always a big mess. Then Mom set some ground rules like no stinky socks on the floor. No food in the room. And no burping in your brother's ear when he's sleeping. Mom's Constitution."

Everyone smiled.

"Exactly," I said. "Like your room, the Constitution gives us the ground rules for the country."

All of a sudden Freedom exclaimed, "I got him!"

She pointed up to a second huge painting on the right side of the room. "There's the guy with the peg leg, and look—he has a sword in front of him."

Freedom quickly took out her sketchbook and flipped through the pages. I noticed a drawing of a horse. She wrote:

> The painting is called The Constitution. *It is by Barry Faulkner. The man with the peg leg is called Gouverneur Morris of Pennsylvania. And we are in the Retunda of the National Archives building.*

"How is this, Mr. Revere? Am I right?" Freedom asked full of excitement.

"Great job, Freedom," I said. Just one change—there should be an *o* in *Rotunda*."

"Rot, Undar, you mean, right, Mr. Revere?" Cam said smiling.

The kids all started moving, heading for the exit.

Freedom's grandfather was standing about ten feet away and waved us over to another glass case.

"Hold on, guys," I said, and gathered the time-traveling Crew together. "You forgot the third amazing document we are here to see. It is called the Bill of Rights, and it is the first ten amendments, or additions, to the U.S. Constitution."

Cam had somehow snuck the yo-yo out of his pocket again, and then put it back. When I was sure Freedom's grandfather could not hear me I said, "All I want you to do is remember this name—George Mason."

Freedom wrote the name down in her sketchbook.

I said, "I think we should go back to 1787 and find out from some exceptional Americans what they were thinking when they created these amazing documents. What do you guys think?"

"A field trip from a field trip?" Tommy asked.

"Exactly right, an adventure within an adventure, with lots to learn and see," I said.

"Oh, okay, I'm in. We just need to get some colonial clothes. I didn't pack any," Tommy said.

"Don't worry, Liberty has some in his saddlebag," I assured him.

"I'm in, too," Cam agreed.

Freedom added, "It sounds like so much fun, I love to time-travel. But I don't want to leave my grandfather."

"We will figure something out, guys," I said.

As we moved through the pristine halls, Cam pulled out his yo-yo and was now doing some tricks. I hoped Liberty had not found any trouble outside.

"Hey, Cam," Tommy whispered. "Can I try your yo-yo?"

"Maybe later," said Cam. "It takes a little practice."

"Hey, I can throw a football like a champ. I bet I can pick this up pretty quick too," Tommy replied.

Before I had a chance to stop him, Tommy tried a difficult trick, and lost control of the yo-yo.

All of a sudden a loud alarm blared through the halls. I stopped in my tracks. Freedom's grandfather grabbed Freedom's hand and ran past me, urging us to follow. Everyone in the building started moving quickly and calm turned to panic.

I looked around and could not see Tommy or Cam. They were just with me. My heart began to race. I started shouting, "Tommy! Cam!"

As people rushed past me and the alarm continued to echo loudly, I looked around nervously wanting Cam and Tommy to appear next to me. I had to do something. I ran over to the metal detectors. A security guard spoke into a radio, giving directions. He looked up at me, suspiciously.

"I am missing two of my students," I said. "They were just with me, but the alarm went off and they vanished. I have no idea where they are."

The guard looked directly at me. "Does one have blond hair and the other brown curly hair? About this tall?" he asked, with a hand out.

"Yes, yes. Have you seen them? Are they okay?" I asked.

"Come with me," he said firmly.

As we rounded a corner, I saw Cam and Tommy sitting on two chairs in a hallway.

"There you are," I said. I was both relieved and worried.

Before they could answer, the security guard said, "It looks like they were having a little too much fun with a yo-yo."

I looked at the boys and shook my head. Just what we need—a national incident.

Tommy said with head lowered, "I was trying a cool trick and I kinda threw the yo-yo into the Rotunda."

"You kinda did what?" I said.

"It had a great spin," Cam said. "I have to give him that."

Turning his attention to me, the guard said, "The yo-yo hit one of the glass cases so hard it caused all of the safety alarms to trigger."

I stood frozen for a second or two not knowing what to say. Did this mean jail for the boys?

"My dad and grandpa are going to be upset with me. They

always tell me I shouldn't show off, but sometimes I can't help it," Tommy said, looking down.

"It was pretty cool, though," Cam said reassuringly, patting Tommy on the shoulder.

"Okay, guys, enough," I said, rather annoyed.

Before too long, the alarms turned off and the boys were allowed to get up from their chairs. After a firm lecture and warning from the security team, along with the confiscation of the yo-yo, we were allowed to leave. Luckily no jail time was required.

"Now that we've caused a major incident at the National Archives, how about we go find Liberty?" I said.

Cam and Tommy shrugged, and followed me out of the building.

"Any chance I could buy a new yo-yo?" Cam asked.

Chapter 9

We left the National Archives building in a hurry. Surprisingly, we found Liberty waiting patiently by the flagpole.

"I was wondering if you were coming back sometime this century," Liberty said, looking perturbed. "I figured you must be in the cafeteria cooking up a buffet of snacks for me, so I decided to wait right here."

"And you stayed right here the whole time, right?" I asked with one eyebrow raised.

"Well, maybe I took a little stroll but you were gone a *really* long time, but no way, no how, did I leave my post for long, Captain."

Cam and Tommy were more quiet than usual, with heads down and hands in their pockets.

Liberty seemed to sense the change in mood. "Wasn't the Constitution amazing? Why all the gloom and doom?"

"It's a long story," Cam replied in a low voice.

"Apparently, I have all day, seeing as you all were in there *forever*," Liberty said. "Wait, where's Freedom and her grandpa?"

"I was just about to ask you the same thing. All was going fine until we had a little yo-yo incident," I said, looking at Tommy and Cam. "Anyway, when the alarms went off Freedom and her grandfather ran past me and we lost them."

"Alarm? In the National Archives? I wonder 'who done it.' I bet it was that woman in the polka-dot dress. No wait, I know—was it Professor Plum with the candlestick?" Liberty said.

"No, it was actually me. I accidentally threw the yo-yo," Tommy said.

"Ouch, that's not good. Anyway," Liberty said, "I'm going to ask Freedom where she is using my mind, one sec." He closed his eyes in an attempt to mentally communicate with Freedom.

After a few seconds of deep thought expressions, Liberty said, "She is okay; she got a little freaked out by the alarms and was just about to mentally text me. They are going for a little walk and will meet us back here in a few minutes . . . Oh, and she said, Tommy, you shouldn't do tricks inside."

Tommy shrugged and said, "Thanks, Freedom."

Something triggered Liberty's memory and he returned to his deep commander voice. "Which secret agent answered my clue correctly?" Liberty asked. "I don't see any written answers. There is a point just waiting to be collected!"

Tommy and Cam frowned. "Um, yeah, well, about that. I'm pretty sure Freedom was first to find the peg leg. She just kinda had to leave in a hurry. Can I have her point for honesty?"

"Nice try, agent . . . but that would be a *no*," Liberty replied sternly, narrowing his eyes dramatically. "Freedom will receive the point when I see her."

Cam shrugged and asked, "Are we still going to find out more about the Constitution or are we pretty much grounded?"

"Ooh, grounded. Good one, Cam, I get it, I get it," Liberty said in a normal tone, nodding his head. "Like the plane is grounded in a storm and can't fly. I'm with you, totally on the same page."

"No one is grounded—*yet*, but like King George, I am feeling the urge to take away your rights," I said sternly.

"Since Freedom and her grandfather are walking, maybe we should time-jump now so it's not too weird we left without them," Tommy said.

"Good idea, Tommy," I replied.

Cam muttered under his breath, just loud enough to hear, "Good one, Tommy, but you're gonna need a lot more good ideas to get us out of the doghouse."

"You're in the doghouse?" Liberty interjected. "Wowza, that is so bad. I mean I'm a horse and I totally wouldn't want to live in the doghouse. Just sayin'. I really like my cable TV."

We quickly followed Liberty to a secluded location. I pulled out the extra colonial clothing from the saddlebag for Tommy and Cam to slip over their modern-day clothes. Soon they were sitting on top of Liberty's saddle. Tommy had his football in his hand so I motioned for him to hide it in Freedom's saddlebag.

"Wait, wait, hold on. I almost forgot the snack you were going to bring me. Could I have it now, please?" Liberty said with his head cocked to one side.

Luckily, I kept a bag of oats in his saddlebag for occasions like this. Liberty took a big bite and began chomping happily. He soon had enough fuel to start the adventure. Now all he had to do was say the magic words and we were off to American history.

Liberty took a big breath and said, "*Rush, rush, rushing to history!*"

Suddenly, a sparkling disk of purple and gold appeared in front of us. It started small but then expanded to the size of a giant hula hoop. As Liberty galloped toward the growing time portal I yelled, "September, 1787. Philadelphia, the Constitutional Convention!" Then I jumped through the portal immediately behind Liberty and the boys.

Instantly, we arrived in the eighteenth century, and I immediately felt the sweltering summer heat. Looking around, I noticed we had landed under the same oak tree where Liberty jumped when we visited Philadelphia in 1776. That was eleven years earlier, when Cam and I witnessed the signing of the Declaration of Independence.

"Whoa," said Cam. "It feels like we just landed on the sun."

"I'm probably going to sound like a nerd," Tommy said, "but I happen to know that the surface of the sun is about ten thousand degrees Fahrenheit. Hey, I like science and sometimes I keep weird bits of trivia in my head."

"We won't hold it against you," said Cam, smirking.

"The Philadelphia Convention took place from May to September 1787," I said. "So I figured if we visited in August we could see everything already in action."

Cam wiped a bead of sweat from his forehead with the back of his sleeve and then clapped a mosquito buzzing in front of his face. "I can handle the heat," said Cam. "But these mosquitos and the smell might kill me."

"No kidding," said Tommy as he slapped a mosquito from his arm. "It smells like rotten eggs mixed with stinky, sweaty socks. Sort of like the Manchester Lions' locker room."

"I don't think it smells that bad," said Liberty.

"Are you kidding?" said Cam.

"Were you raised in a barn?"

"Actually, yes, I was," said Liberty, proudly.

"Is a barn better than a doghouse?" Cam asked. Liberty nodded.

"Let's not forget why we are here," I said. "To meet the Founders of our country and learn more about how they wrote the Constitution of the United States of America and the Bill of Rights."

"Wait, the one we just saw at the National Archives?" Cam asked.

"Yes, the very one," I said.

"This is really cool, Mr. Revere. I love to time-travel, plus there's no way I can bump into Elizabeth in the past," Tommy said energetically.

"Is your girlfriend still trying to hang with you?" teased Cam.

"She is *not* my girlfriend," said Tommy. "Elizabeth is barely a friend. But she does cheer for our football team, so I need to be sort of nice to her."

"Yeah, and she is really mean to Freedom, and called her Free-*dumb*, remember?" Cam said.

"I don't like the way she treats Freedom, either, but we need cheerleaders, okay? And she can be kinda nice at times," Tommy said.

"Sharks can be nice, too, but that doesn't mean I'm going to swim with one," Cam teased.

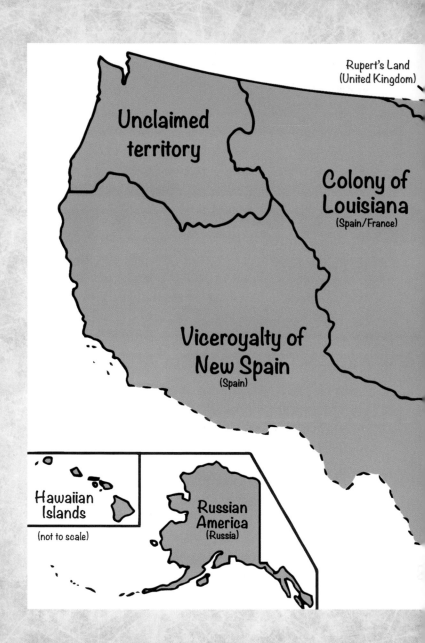

Disputed between Massachusetts and
Colony of New Brunswick (UK)

Disputed between Northwest Territory
and Rupert's Land (UK)

New
Hampshire

Vermont
Republic

Connecticut
Western
Reserve

Erie
Triangle

New
York

Massachusetts

Rhode
Island

Connecticut

New Jersey

Delaware

Maryland

Northwest
Territory

Pennsylvania

Virginia

Unorganized
territory

North
Carolina

South
Carolina

Georgia

States
Territories
Other countries
Disputed areas

East Florida
(Spain)

Disputed between
United States
and West Florida

West Florida
(Spain)

States and Territories of the United States of America
1790

"Good point," Tommy agreed.

As we made our way to Main Street I could see that Philadelphia had definitely grown in size since our last visit. On every side there were bustling shops.

"Out of the way, before you get run over!" a carriage driver shouted at us, then splashed us with muddy water. He turned down a narrow curving street, cursing us all the way. A chicken ran past, and after it a craggy dog that looked up at us quizzically.

"I'm no genius, but I'm pretty sure those pigs aren't helping with the smells around here," Cam said as he scrunched up his nose. One particularly large pig eyed us as if we were in the middle of his farm.

Where are we going exactly? I wondered. Feeling that we were completely lost I pulled out a map. We needed to find Independence Hall, located between Fifth and Sixth Streets. Following the map, we turned right on Chestnut Street.

"Pee-ew," said Liberty.

"I thought you said the smell doesn't bother you," Cam said.

"It doesn't," Liberty replied.

"Then why did you say pee-yew?" asked Tommy. "Y'know, Liberty, that's what people say when something smells bad, right?"

"Oh," nodded Liberty. "Well, that's not what I meant. When you pointed out all the pigs roaming the streets it made me think of PU, the letter *P* and the letter *U* for Pigs Union. Seriously, back on the farm the pigs thought they owned the place. And if they didn't get enough slop or if they didn't have enough mud they'd all go on strike and just walk around passing gas and stinking everything up."

Liberty never ceased to make me smile. "Well, that certainly explains the smell," I said, rolling my eyes. "But I think we should also consider the fact that there are about forty thousand people living here right now. In fact, currently Philadelphia is America's largest city. And most of its population is concentrated within these eight blocks, which includes an open sewer system."

As we walked along the road to Fifth Street, we became covered in dusty sweat. Tommy and Cam kept swatting flies and mosquitos that buzzed around their faces and necks. "Did anyone bring any mosquito repellent? I feel like I'm being eaten alive," said Tommy.

I almost fell over a pot on an open fire in the middle of the sidewalk.

"Watch out for me chicken cookin'!" a hunched woman with red hair shouted at us, waving her arms. We picked up our pace.

Liberty swatted a dozen flies out of the air with a single swish of his tail. "Too bad you don't have an awesome tail like mine. I never leave home without it."

"Here," I said as I reached into Liberty's saddlebag. "Spray some of this on you. But do it quickly so we don't call attention to ourselves." Luckily we were wearing colonial clothes or we would have stood out more than we already did.

Even though Philadelphia was the largest city in the country at the time, there were no tall skyscrapers like in a modern-day city. It was mostly rows of houses with little space between them, stacked together two or three stories tall. It felt like a busy small town, but there were no honking horns. Just dusty roads filled with carriages. As we walked down the street we passed shops, including a butcher and a soapmaker.

"Look up ahead, that is Independence Hall," I said, pointing.

"The very building where the Founders debated the Constitution." I could see the familiar spire of the famous building in the distance. Its red brick could be seen above the other buildings.

"You mean the one with the tall tower thing on top?" Tommy asked.

"Yes, the tall structure on top of the building that points toward the sky is actually called a spire. They are usually found on churches," I replied.

A large clock faced outward on the spire above two sets of windows. In front of Independence Hall sat a large dirt and grass park.

"So what or who exactly are we looking for?" asked Cam.

"I'm hoping to find James Madison. Mr. Madison was a vital part of the writing of the Constitution and Bill of Rights. I would really love for you to be able to meet him. Liberty, do you think you could help us out by using your time-travel senses?"

Liberty shut his eyes and concentrated. He mumbled something like, "James Madison, Father of the Constitution, ice cream and Popsicles and a cold glass of lemonade and . . ."

"Liberty!" I blurted, snapping him out of his trance. "You're supposed to be looking for James Madison, remember?"

"Oh, yeah, sorry, Captain," Liberty said. "I think I could concentrate harder and find Mr. Madison if I had a cold beverage or a scoop of carrot ice cream."

"Carrot ice cream?" asked Tommy with the kind of look that someone gives when they've just heard a really bad idea.

Ignoring both of them, I said, "If my historical notes are accurate, James Madison should be staying at Mary's boardinghouse. Liberty, if I get you something refreshing could you get us to the boardinghouse?"

BACK *of the* STATE HOUSE, PHILADELPHIA.

This is the back of the Pennsylvania State House in the year 1799.
It is known as Independence Hall, where delegates met to sign
the Declaration of Independence and later to debate the U.S. Constitution.

"Now you're talking," said Liberty, smiling. "It's about a block north on Fifth Street."

I stared at him, suspiciously, and said, "That did not seem to take you much effort."

Liberty shrugged. "It's amazing how much better my time-travel senses work with the right motivation."

Oh brother, I thought, as I reached into his saddlebag, took out a big, juicy apple, and fed it to him.

The boys laughed.

"Hey guys, before we go on Liberty's wild goose chase to find James Madison, gather round so I can give you a quick summary of what is going on right now in American history," I said.

"Goose chase? I take offense to that," Liberty added.

We found a place in the shade to huddle and I pulled out a map and some notes.

"So, right now, we are in the year 1787. I know this is a little confusing, but the Americans declared independence from Great Britain in 1776. Even though they declared independence, the war lasted until 1783. As you know, George Washington led the American Army courageously for all those years."

Always in the mood for a spontaneous quiz, I asked the Crew, "Do you know what happened between 1783 and this year, 1787?"

"Um," Cam said, "Philadelphia grew like crazy and they all came back here for the Constitution?"

I laughed. "Yes indeed, very good short summary, Cam, but there is more. In the years between 1783 and 1787, after the war was finally over, the young country of America was pulling itself apart. There were thirteen united American states at the time but each one had its own way of doing business. Each state wanted to run things its own way even though they all were in favor of being free from King George."

"It sounds like there were a lot of cooks in the kitchen," Liberty added. "Just a little kitchen lingo for you, in case you forgot about snack time. Have we put any thought into that?"

"This kinda sounds like our dodgeball team. If we all ran around with no leader and all did our own thing we really wouldn't be too good of a team," Cam said.

"Luckily, we had you," Tommy said, giving Cam a fist bump.

"Yes, Cam, you are entirely right. At the time, the American team wasn't that strong because it was not really working together," I replied.

"You mean like the Americans were wearing the American team jersey but weren't really using the same playbook?" Tommy asked.

"Yes, exactly right. You guys are on the ball. Spending some time with the security guards at the National Archives building seems to have done you some good," I said, winking. I could not help myself. "One of the men fighting for a more unified American team was James Madison. How about we find him and ask him why," I said.

I put my map and notes away, and we made our way from our cool spot under the tree back onto the Philadelphia streets in search of the Father of the Constitution, James Madison.

"Liberty, we should really get you one of those carriages. It would be much more fun for you to pull us around than all this walking," Tommy said. His forehead was nearly covered in sweat and he had rolled up his colonial shirtsleeves.

"Oh no, I refuse to be a horse and buggy show," Liberty replied, shaking his head. "I mean, I got the horse part down, but no way on the buggy."

"Back to Operation Find James Madison. Are you concentrating, Liberty?" I asked.

"Ohhhh, I like that name, it makes us sound very official. Like we are Navy SEALs. Wait, maybe we should be detectives on a secret case," Liberty said.

I laughed and said, "Where does your keen sense of direction tell us to go next?"

"Um, let me see. I sense that James Madison is very close. But the heat is making it difficult to pinpoint his exact location."

"That would make sense. I mean it is ten thousand degrees outside," Cam teased.

Thinking out loud, Liberty said, "He's not at the boarding-house."

We were walking slowly down the street having no idea what was about to happen.

Suddenly, a chubby man in a white apron came bolting out of a shop door, bouncing along and frantically waving a long stick of French bread.

"Thieves, thieves, stop zem!" the man shouted in a strong French accent, "Zey stole my best croissants!" He was looking left and right rapidly. Out of the corner of my eye, I saw three boys escape down a back alley.

We stood on the corner across the street trying to absorb what was happening. Tommy and Cam looked at me, wondering what was going on.

Then the Frenchman turned to us—"There! There are ze little rapscallions, arrest zem!"

Uh-oh, he had mistaken Tommy and Cam for the bread thieves.

He started to chase after us, French bread loaf raised, shouting, "If I catch you I will beat you wiz my hand!"

"We better get out of here. He isn't messing around," Liberty said.

"Man, I thought it was innocent until proven guilty. That's what all of the cop shows say," Cam said nervously. He pulled himself up onto Liberty as the Frenchman stumbled across the street toward us. Tommy was able to jump halfway up when Liberty started moving.

Luckily, the Frenchman looked like he ate quite a few pastries and did not spend much time at the gym. In the distance we saw his face getting redder and redder.

"I will get you!" he shouted as we disappeared around a corner.

We kept running and riding for about six more blocks. When I felt we were safe, the boys jumped off Liberty and we sat on a bench.

"Let me catch my breath, and I'll go get us some drinks from that store over there and be right back," I said, still panting. When I returned we drank our drinks and rested.

After a few minutes I said, "Back to the search for James Madison. Liberty, I know most of the delegates to the Constitutional Convention did their work in taverns and private homes, all within walking distance of the Pennsylvania State House, better known as Independence Hall."

"Let me put that in my thinking hat . . . Tavern . . . beep, beep, beep," Liberty said, making machine sounds with his mouth. "Nope, I don't think he's there," Liberty said.

"So, basically we have no clue," Cam said.

"Wait, wait, hold that thought. I smell coffee, which makes me think of donuts, which makes me think of Munchkins, which makes me think . . ." Liberty rambled.

"Liberty, focus. What does the coffee mean?" I asked.

"I am focused, Revere. Great detectives can't make decisions willy-nilly," Liberty replied. "I am sensing he may be at the coffee shop as we speak. In fact, he is right over there."

Ten feet from where we were sitting there was a sign that read COFFEE.

"Liberty, are you telling me that we just ran six blocks and just happen to be outside the coffee shop where James Madison is located?"

"Hmm, that appears to be correct. Once again the case has been solved using my super sleuth skills," Liberty said, winking.

I shook my head as we made our way up the steps to the coffee shop and through the doors.

"So, is this like the first Starbucks or Dunkin' Donuts, Mr. Revere?" Cam asked.

"If so, can I get a Mocha Frappuccino and a glazed donut?" Tommy added.

I smiled. "Well, Starbucks and Dunkin' Donuts did not come around until the twentieth century, so not exactly. But these are the coffee shops that came before those. Unfortunately, there is no Frappuccino, just regular old coffee."

Inside the coffee shop, it was quiet at this time of day, like a library. The only sounds we could hear were mumbled discussions from the street and the sound of dishes being washed.

"That man looks like he's concentrating on something big. He kinda reminds me of my grandfather when he's studying his stocks," Tommy said.

In the corner, I noticed a man sitting alone at a table near an open window, hunched over his papers. He was moving his mouth in a quiet, thoughtful way as he scribbled notes.

From my pocket, I pulled out a picture of an old painting of James Madison and looked at it before handing it to Cam.

Do you recognize this exceptional American?
He is the "Father of the Constitution," James Madison.

Cam looked carefully at the picture and then at the man and said, "That's him! We found our suspect."

Seeing James Madison in person was like seeing a famous celebrity or athlete. It was hard to imagine this was him in the flesh. Unlike George Washington, however, Madison looked like he was hiding in the corner, his body language saying "please don't disturb me."

I was not exactly sure what to do and was a little nervous with all the questions I had to ask, but figured I had to make the move and introduce ourselves. Tommy, Cam, and I walked over to the table.

"Mr. Madison?" I asked.

He looked up nervously, then quickly glanced at the three of us, but hesitated to respond.

For a second I was concerned we had the wrong man. Even though he was sitting down I could tell he was really small in stature. He held a pen delicately. This is not what I expected. When we met Samuel Adams, Paul Revere, and Dr. Warren, they made a strong impression. Samuel Adams was very grumpy but pulled off the Boston Tea Party in glorious fashion. James Madison, on the other hand, seemed very anxious. Could this really be the man who would one day be known as the "Father of the Constitution"? Looks can be deceiving, I thought.

There was a long pause as we looked at each other. Finally, he said, "Uh, yes, I am James Madison, and you are?"

I paused, in awe, until Cam bumped my elbow and whispered, "Mr. Revere, you were saying?"

"Oh, yes, sorry," I said. "I am Rush Revere, history teacher, and these are my students, Cam and Tommy."

They both smiled widely but Mr. Madison was completely quiet. It was almost painful to stand there. I was so excited to meet him, but I did not want to make any errors. The silence went on so long, in fact, that I began to turn around, my face warm with nervousness. Certainly this was not Patrick Henry loudly playing his fiddle. Maybe he did not want to be disturbed?

I tried to leave with grace and said, "Mr. uh, thank you . . ."

But before I could finish Tommy leaned in and said to Mr. Madison, "Hey, what are you reading?"

Mr. Madison replied sheepishly, "I, um, am reading books about history," and then returned to the huge book he had in front of him. It felt awkward to me, but Tommy did not seem bothered. Nor for that matter did Cam. Both were looking at Madison with a curious expression on their faces. In a way, his quietness seemed to let them into his world.

I counted ten books spread out in front of James Madison; three were open and filled with tiny little notes. He pulled at his hair and mumbled something in a near whisper. Tommy leaned in to hear.

What seemed like minutes passed by as Madison looked up from his papers to Tommy and then his eyes darted shyly to us and down to his books.

"We were looking for you!" Tommy said loudly. Madison appeared to nearly jump out of his seat. He looked like he wanted to crawl into his book.

"Oh, you were looking for me? I think you are confusing me with someone else," Madison said.

"Nope," Cam said. "You are the guy we are looking for, James Madison of Virginia."

"Oh," James Madison said quietly.

"Hey, I have a question for you, sir, if you have a second," Tommy said bravely.

I was the one who was speechless. Tommy and Cam were speaking to one of the founders of our country, a celebrity, and they were doing all the talking. I was bouncing from one foot to the other.

"Oh, yes, I will try to answer if able, young man," Madison said, appearing more relaxed.

"You said you were reading about history. Why are you doing that?" Cam asked.

Madison looked excited for the first time and said, "Well, I have been working on this all morning. I am trying to figure it out. This stack of books contains information on governments by philosophers and politicians from history. I will continue to read until I feel confident about what to do."

I was so excited that I jumped in and asked, "Could we ask you a few questions about the Constitution of the United States of America?"

Mr. Madison looked surprised and suddenly nervous again, "I . . . I should get back to my reading," he said, politely. He looked back down at his books.

I wanted to kick myself. I knew that George Washington kept the Convention in the strictest secrecy. Even with the summer heat the Convention windows were all closed, except for one, so no one could overhear. Had I ruined our chance to find out more about the Constitution?

At that moment, Liberty poked his head through the open window closest to our table and leaned so far in that his chin whiskers and lower lip touched Mr. Madison's hair like someone giving him a sloppy kiss. In pure shock, he stumbled sideways in his chair and his papers flew everywhere. Deftly, Tommy caught Mr. Madison's shoulder and pushed him back so all four legs of the chair were once again on the wooden floor.

I looked at Liberty, stunned. I was afraid James Madison would be upset, but he looked kindly at Liberty and patted him softly on the nose. "Oh, hello, Mr. Horse," he said. "You're a curious one, aren't you?" I remembered the effect Liberty had on George Washington. The General even wanted to recruit Liberty into the Continental Army. This was different, though. Madison looked at Liberty like he was speaking only to him, and Liberty smiled sweetly back.

"I apologize, Mr. Madison," I said. "This happens to be my horse, Liberty."

The future President raised his eyebrows and said, "Liberty, what a fine name," and patted him on the nose.

Liberty lowered his head for a nice scratch. Mr. Madison was standing now and was indeed a short man, no taller than about five feet, five inches. Without saying anything, Mr. Madison began to organize his books. He took his coffee cup with slumped shoulders to the bar, and smiled nicely at the bartender. When he came back he piled all his books up and looked like he would crumble under the weight.

Without saying a word, the Father of the Constitution turned to go, out of our lives forever. I had blown it.

"Uh-oh, Mr. Revere, maybe we should practice being a little more stealthy about the Constitution. It's kind of top secret, right?" Cam whispered into my ear.

Just then, Mr. Madison reached out his hand with a soft handshake for Tommy and Cam and me, and gave Liberty a small candy he had in his pocket.

Then, as he turned to walk out the door he said quietly, "I am having dinner with some of my friends in a few hours. If you would like to come, we will be dining at Mary's boardinghouse at four." And with that, he left.

"Score," said Cam. "We're going to have dinner with James Madison!"

"What are we going to do before that?" asked Tommy. "My phone says it's only three o'clock."

I explained, "It's common during this time in history to have two large meals during the day, a late breakfast and an early dinner," I said. "We eat at four o'clock."

Liberty suddenly appeared behind us and asked, "Did someone say *early dinner?* Because I'm famished."

This is Independence Hall in Philadelphia in modern day.
Can you see the American flag flying above it?

Chapter 5

I was so excited by the thought of dinner with James Madison, I completely forgot about the crazy French shop owner. We casually walked out of the coffee shop and stood in the street discussing our next moves.

"I've got to add this to Grandpa's notebook. He will never believe me but I know he loves our Founding Fathers and thinks they were really smart," Tommy said.

"Great idea. I am sure he will be so excited to read your notes when we get back," I said.

Tommy began to pull out his notebook and pencil.

"Zere you are. You come over here right now!" a voice shouted. We turned around to see the man in the white apron, angrily waving a stick of French bread, yelling from the doorway of his shop.

"I think we better get out of here pronto, Mr. Revere," Cam said.

"Where's Liberty?" asked Tommy, looking around.

I was unsure myself. Last I saw him, he was poking his head through the coffee shop window.

"Hurry, boys, follow me, and keep close," I said, racing away from the coffee shop. "Let's head that way."

Our escape seemed like a marathon with the crazy French bread man screaming behind us.

Cam pointed. "Look, is that Liberty?" he asked.

We all turned in the direction Cam was pointing and sure enough, there was Liberty standing next to a wooden cart of fresh vegetables. A woman in a long colonial brown dress was patting him and looking at him adoringly. I could have sworn I saw a ribbon peeking out from the top of his mane.

Liberty, you charmer, I thought to myself. He was clearly trying to finagle a carrot or two.

We ran over and wrestled him away from the vegetable cart, reminding him of our important operation.

"Yes, yes, Captain. I was just taking a little break," Liberty said. "You know what they say, taking a vegetable break now and then is good for the soul."

"Who is 'they'?" I asked, continuing before he could answer. "We need to head over to Mary's boardinghouse on Fifth Street. We do not have time to sit around here and chomp."

"Besides, the French bread man will be hot on our trail," Cam added. "I think he has kid radar."

"I agree with Tommy," Liberty said. "Why sit around when we can pick something up to go? I'm thinking a McDonald's drive-through."

"There's a McDonald's around here?" Tommy joked. "I could go for some Chicken McNuggets."

"See, Tommy, you are a man after my own heart. Except I would go for a fresh salad but hold the mayo," Liberty added.

Realizing this banter could go on forever, I said, "Okay, we should just make our way to the boardinghouse. We can grab a snack on the way. Liberty, could you lead us there?"

"Your wish is my command. It just so happens I was studying a 1787 map of Philadelphia while you were yucking it up with James Madison," Liberty said.

Something told me Liberty's map studying was unlikely.

"Okay, great, Mary's boardinghouse, here we come," I said.

"Mr. Revere, is a boardinghouse sort of like a hotel in the eighteenth century?" Tommy asked.

"It's more like a bed-and-breakfast," I replied. "It is usually a family home where people rent one or more rooms. In fact, James Madison stayed there for three years during the Continental Congress. His real home was in Virginia. But Mary's boardinghouse became his home away from home."

Eventually, we made our way through the city to Fifth Street.

"Liberty, I trust you will avoid trouble as always," I said with a smile. We left him near a brick building and water trough.

Liberty nodded and squinted his eyes as if he were listening intently.

We entered Mary's boardinghouse and saw James Madison on the first floor in the main dining room. He was sitting at a wooden table in front of a fireplace. Of course, it was too hot outside to need a fire. The table was set with a loaf of sliced bread at the center. We could barely see Mr. Madison, as his books were stacked high. His hands danced over the pages as he wrote notes. There were people all around the boardinghouse talking and laughing, but Mr. Madison sat alone, quietly. He seemed deep in thought.

"Mr. Revere, should we go back outside and knock or ring a doorbell or something? It seems kinda rude to barge in," Tommy said in a low voice. "My grandpa always said you should announce yourself. Probably so I wouldn't sneak up and scare him, but still."

I took Tommy's advice and announced to the room, "Mr. Madison, it is Rush Revere and students."

"Hello," said Mr. Madison, in a soft voice, lifting his head from his notes. "Come in." He motioned for us to get closer. Then he put his stack of books on the side tables next to him, clearing off his own.

"I spoke with General George Washington about a few things as I walked back here from the coffeehouse," James Madison said. "When I mentioned your name, he remembered you and your students from the American Revolution. He said you had an incredible horse."

Cam looked at me, titling his head to one side and nodding in agreement. "George Washington remembers us, eh? Not bad, not bad," he whispered.

"Thank you so much, Mr. Madison," I said. "He and Liberty did have quite a connection."

At this, James Madison offered a small smile. "Furthermore, General Washington is very appreciative of your support of our country at Lexington, Concord, and Bunker Hill. In fact, he said he was so impressed with you and your students that his rule on secrecy for the Constitutional Convention could be lifted for you."

I felt so honored that these exceptional patriots trusted us.

Speaking to James Madison was like speaking to a Hall of Fame baseball player, great musician, or savvy businessperson. He seemed larger than life.

"Thank you, Mr. Madison," I uttered, full of excitement, "but I was simply an observer there to learn and teach my students."

A few ladies and gentlemen joined us as we gathered around the table. Tommy sat closest to James Madison, and followed his every move.

After Mr. Madison offered a silent prayer, we began to eat quietly. The food was surprisingly delicious—roasted chicken, corn on the cob, and assorted vegetables filled our plates. It wasn't McDonald's Chicken McNuggets but Tommy and Cam did not seem to mind, digging into their potatoes. They pushed the roasted rabbit to the side of their plates, though. As the courses were served, we sat mostly in silence.

Finally Cam said, "Mr. Madison, it is really hot in Philadelphia. Why are you all here? Don't you want to be at home with your families?"

Mr. Madison slowly looked up from his plate and replied, "Yes, young man, I would certainly rather be home in Virginia. But the country is in great need. We are pulling ourselves apart day by day."

I could see the motor in Cam's mind spinning, trying to figure out the meaning of Mr. Madison's words.

Slowly James Madison rose from his seat and waited for everyone to quiet down. He said to the table, "During the American Revolution, Virginia and the other twelve colonies united to fight Great Britain and King George III. Unfortunately, now, eleven years later, each colony is more interested in its own pursuits than those of the whole union."

A man with a deep voice stood and spoke from across the table: "If we are not careful we will lose all the freedoms for which we desperately fought."

"True, true," another voice from the table said loudly.

Something clicked for Tommy and he said, "But the Americans are all on the same team. Why don't they just play together? It seems pretty easy to me."

"Good question," I said.

"If only it could be so easy, Tommy," Madison said. "You are right, the American states are technically on the same team. However, since independence, the different leaders in each state cannot agree. They think the central government is like a king, taking away their freedoms."

The man with the deep voice wobbled as he stood up from the table and shouted, "Those scoundrels!" He swung out his arms, tipping over a water jug, and it spilled all over the table.

Cam and Tommy nudged each other and started laughing. Then Cam blurted out, "Does anyone have any paper towels?"

I gave them the eye and quickly changed the subject.

With some hesitation, I raised my voice and said to the table, "Would it not be better for the states to unify to protect themselves from other nations that want to take away their freedoms?"

"Hear, hear!" slurred the deep-voiced man. His cheeks were red.

Mr. Madison looked at the man for a second, then said, "That does seem the best course, Mr. Revere, but strong leaders in each state, with various motivations, do not agree."

Tommy leaned over and whispered, "I totally get it. It would be like putting Elizabeth and the cheerleaders in charge of

Manchester Middle School and letting them make decisions for everyone else. Trouble," he said, rolling his eyes.

"Yeah, give Elizabeth any power and she thinks she is queen bee," Cam added. "I bet she would get rid of the art class first. And then she would force Tommy to eat lunch with her *every* day."

"She already tries to do that now," Tommy said.

The boys looked up from their private conversation to see the table was silent again. The others were quietly waiting for them to finish. Mr. Madison was looking at them confused.

After a pause he asked, "Have you boys heard of the Articles of Confederation?" Both boys sat up and shook their heads, nervously.

Madison said, "The Articles of Confederation is our current system of government. It began six years ago, in 1781. The thirteen new states realized they needed some form of government to act together against any new threats. The Articles of Confederation do not make a strong government, however, and there are many serious issues."

I asked, "Are you in favor of or opposed to the Articles of Confederation?"

Cam looked at me with a sideways glance as if to say, "Good one."

"I am partly opposed. The Articles of Confederation agreement is unfortunately too weak to ensure we survive as a united country. It unites us, but not enough. We are weak, and a weak government does not survive," Madison replied.

Tommy raised his hand and said with excitement, "Mr. Madison, I think I get what you're saying. The Articles of Confederation basically invite all thirteen states to live under one roof.

They each get their own bedroom and get to make their own laws for their own room. But what you need now are *house rules* so all the states do their chores like paying taxes so we can have the things that we all use and need, like the military, the police, and roads."

James Madison smiled like he had just seen a beautiful sunrise. "That is correct, Tommy. In fact, brilliant. You must make your parents so proud."

"My grandpa always tells me you have to obey your parents' rules when you live under their roof," Tommy said.

"Your grandfather is correct," Mr. Madison said, nodding. "So, in the simplest terms, those of us from Virginia are here in Philadelphia to propose that a new Constitution be written to replace the weak Articles of Confederation."

I nodded enthusiastically. It was thrilling to witness the logic behind one of the most extraordinary creations in history, the U.S. Constitution.

"It sounds like you have done the most research and have the best plan, Mr. Madison," Cam said. "Why not just tell the other states to agree and move on? Sounds totally like a plan to me."

Madison smiled, looking around the table. "If it were that simple, son, I would already be heading back to my farm in Virginia. However, we are creating something that has never existed before in the world—a government of the people. Very brave and smart men disagree on how best to preserve our freedoms. That is why we are here in Philadelphia, to debate and determine the best plan of action."

I was in complete awe of Madison's intelligence and ability to capture Cam and Tommy's attention despite his shyness. To create a new government of the people was simply incredible. I hoped the boys were absorbing every second.

Before Mr. Madison could continue, there was a loud crash in the courtyard. Mr. Madison seemed startled and raced over to the window. Cam followed. After looking out the window, Cam turned around and shook his head.

"Um, I think Liberty is trying to take a bath," Cam said.

Mr. Madison could not believe his eyes. Liberty was splashing with his hooves in a large pail of water next to a parked carriage.

"Your horse has more personality than our entire Convention combined," Mr. Madison said with a smile.

I excused myself from the table and went outside to see exactly what Liberty was doing.

"Oh, helloooo, Revere. Fancy meeting you here," Liberty said, continuing to splash.

"May I ask what you are doing, besides interrupting one of the most important conversations we have ever had?" I said.

"Interrupting? I'm just out here minding my own business. Except I was baking in the sun," Liberty said. "And I don't mean baking cookies, although some oatmeal cookies sound really good about now. Anyway, what is a horse to do when all of the shady trees are taken? So, I improvised with this mini-bath."

"What was that crash? You scared James Madison," I asked.

"Oh, that. Well, you see I was trying to carry the pail in my teeth by its handle. You know, to make a shower next to this parked carriage. But the handle broke and the pail hit the ground, sooooooo I kinda had to change plans on the fly," Liberty explained.

I rolled my eyes knowing I would get nowhere trying to understand Liberty's logic.

"Could you try to keep it down for a little while longer? Mr. Madison is just about to tell us about the Virginia Plan," I said.

"Ohhhh, well, since you put it that way, yes, yes sirree, Bob," Liberty said, making an attempt at a salute.

I went back inside. James Madison was bending down to remove a piece of paper from a locked chest. "I trust you all not to say a word of this to anyone. It is very important that we keep our plans private, until we are ready to share them with the people at large."

We all nodded in agreement.

"Scouts' honor," Tommy said saluting with his left hand.

James Madison smiled and nodded at him, looking somewhat confused.

"I have been working on this Virginia Plan for months. I have read philosophy and books on government throughout American history. This is the initial sketch of the plan that we proposed at the Convention." He pointed to his piece of paper. "Essentially, we are proposing a new system of government where the American people rule, instead of the King."

"How do the people rule?" Tommy asked, innocently looking around the table. He seemed unsure if this was a dumb question.

Madison kindly and softly replied, "Well, Tommy, to put it simply, in our Virginia Plan, we are proposing three branches of government. One of the branches, the legislative branch, would be made up of representatives from each state."

"So those representatives would be the voice of the people?" Cam asked, also appearing uncertain of his understanding. "Kind of like a class leader at our school?"

"Yes, Cam, well done. Like your friend Elizabeth if I remember correctly?" Mr. Madison said. "The legislative branch would bring the voice of the people to the government. Every American citizen would be heard in every decision and new law."

"Wow!" I shouted. I did not mean to say it out loud. The whole table turned toward me, and I felt my cheeks turn red.

Cam saved the awkwardness by asking, "So, why do we need three branches? It seems like the legislative branch is enough."

"Very perceptive, young man. We believe if there are three branches of government we will ensure no one person or group has too much power," Mr. Madison replied. "Each branch will be a *check* on the power of the other branch. This is the best way to preserve the rights of the people."

"What would the other two do?" Cam asked, curiously.

Madison replied, "The legislative branch creates laws, and as the people elect the representatives, they bring the voice of the people to the government. The executive branch carries out the laws created by the legislative branch. And, finally, the judicial branch reviews laws created by the legislative branch. Basically, there is a separation of power, where one branch does not do everything. That way, one group cannot gain too much power."

Tommy raised his hand and said, "Mr. Madison, I agree with Cam. Why not just go in there tomorrow and tell them your Virginia Plan is best and just get them to sign now? Call it a day."

Madison smiled and said, "Thank you, young man, for the vote of confidence. I must say I am a nervous public speaker at times. I often lose track of my thoughts and have been told that I mumble. In my head the words are perfect, but much is lost when I give a speech. It is an affliction that often inhibits my confidence."

Tommy looked at me and then back at the guests around the table. Then he stood up. He crouched as if he were in the middle of a football game about to receive the ball from the center. "It sounds like my last football game," he said. "It was fourth down and we were inches from the goal line. Everyone on the team had a different idea about how to win. Run the ball, pass the ball, or go for a field goal. I mean, everyone was throwing out ideas. It was really confusing."

Madison and the entire table looked at Tommy as if they had no idea what he was describing. I heard lots of chattering around the table, words like *football, center,* and *field goal.* Of course football was not yet invented in 1787.

Cam looked a bit puzzled and asked, "So if the other colonies don't like your Virginia Plan, what exactly do they want to do?"

Mr. Madison replied, "The crux of the matter is a fight between large and small states and representation in the legislative branch. In our Virginia Plan, we are suggesting two different *chambers* or sections. One chamber has an even number of representatives per state, and the other has a number of representatives based on the state's population.

"The small states including New Jersey are not happy with this. They say that states with a larger population will rule, and this is not fair," Mr. Madison said.

"What does New Jersey propose?" I asked, knowing this was a very important part of the Convention debate.

"New Jersey's plan is to have one chamber in the legislative branch and one vote per state regardless of size," Madison replied, without a moment's pause. He knew every detail immediately.

The man with the deep voice was shifting from side to side, eyes half-closed.

James Madison went on to explain to the table that the big states thought it was unfair for the small states to have the same number of representatives. The big states thought they had more people and should have more of a voice.

Just then another loud crash came echoing from the courtyard. Tommy and Cam both laughed uproariously. I guessed Liberty was up to something. Luckily, Madison seemed too lost in thought to notice the disruption.

"Sounds like you guys need to lock the doors until you figure it out," Tommy said.

Madison smiled, seeming comfortable and nowhere near as shy as when we first met. "It is funny you should say that. All the doors, windows, and curtains have been closed for secrecy reasons and it very hot and muggy in the Assembly Room."

"You mean the Assembly Sauna," Cam joked.

Madison stood and said, "We should enter the living room where the chairs are a bit more comfortable."

We all rose from the table and followed Madison to a room with formal sofas and chairs. As we did, I glanced out the window to the courtyard and did not see Liberty. I could only imagine what he was doing.

"So what will you do, Mr. Madison?" I asked, respectfully.

"I am not altogether happy with the events of the Convention so far, but I feel we are close to an agreement. If we can make a compromise, neither the Virginia Plan nor the New Jersey plan will be approved in full," Madison said.

"But a compromise seems like it would be fair to no one, and everyone would lose," Tommy said.

Madison smiled again and said softly, "Possibly, but the country will win, and our primary objective is to create a new constitution that will benefit the *people* of the United States of America. That must always come first. The state of Connecticut has proposed a plan that could be acceptable to all the states."

Cam started raising his hand frantically as if he were on a game show.

"Oh, can I guess what Connecticut is proposing?" Cam asked.

I was thrilled with his confidence and willingness to take a stab at an answer.

Madison, although shy at first, seemed to inspire the boys, just like George Washington had. "Sure you may, son, but it is rather complicated," Mr. Madison replied.

"Son?" Cam whispered to me with a twinkle in his eye. "George Washington remembers us and James Madison called me son. We are on a roll."

I laughed at another keen observation.

"Actually, I think it is better you tell us on this one. I think I know, but I'm not really sure," Cam said, seeming to lose his nerve. "I was just thinking since Connecticut is a small state they probably want one representative per state or something like that."

"Yes, you are on the right track. To be brief, Connecticut is also proposing a legislative branch with two chambers. The first is called the House of Representatives, with representation based on the state's population. The second chamber, the Senate, would allow each state to have two representatives regardless of population."

"I bet everyone will agree on this one," Tommy said, winking at me. Of course, he knew that we currently have a Senate and House of Representatives, so it was a good bet. What Tommy did not yet know was that the fight at the Convention was not yet over and the long, hot summer would continue with two major issues: slavery and the Bill of Rights.

"I must say, your students are a joy to spend time with. One day, I see them representing the American people," Madison said. He stood up as the boys smiled at each other.

We took this as our cue to politely leave dinner. I gave a signal to the boys and we all stood.

"Thank you, Mr. Madison, for the most incredible dinner and conversation. I simply don't have the words to describe what it means to us," I said.

"You are most welcome. Thank you for allowing me to synthesize my thoughts verbally. Tomorrow, when the Convention reconvenes, I believe I know how to move forward," Madison said and shook our hands.

We all smiled and said goodbye to the group.

"If you are still in town, you should come by Independence Hall. I will make special arrangements for you to observe part of the session," Mr. Madison said.

I could barely believe my ears. Before I had the chance to absorb the invitation, Tommy said, "Yes, we will be there. We can't wait!"

Chapter 6

We walked out of the boardinghouse into the muggy air, hoping to find Liberty waiting nearby. A misty hot haze rose from the cobblestones, as horse-drawn carriages clomped past. Since we had an early dinner, it was still light outside.

"Where is Liberty?" Tommy asked, repeating the familiar phrase.

We looked left and right but could not find him.

"Let's wait here for a minute in this spot of shade until he turns up. It should be any day now," I said smiling.

"Mr. Madison is really awesome. He reminds me of my grandpa," Tommy said with a look of wonder in his eye. "Madison is always focused and explains things in a simple way. At first he was shy but when he talked about the Convention he made it really interesting."

"You are exactly right, Tommy," I replied.

Cam added, "I thought it was a lot of pressure being the head of the dodgeball team, but that's nothing compared to trying to get all the states to agree on a new constitution. That's crazy pressure."

"You are entirely right, Cam," I said. "If you were James Madison, what would you be thinking tonight, before the Convention resumes tomorrow? Imagine trying to come up with a plan that everyone will be happy with, while not sacrificing your own principles. It is remarkable how many late nights and long hours James Madison worked for the good of the country. The freedoms we know today are based largely on his efforts."

"I thought you said something about going to see the Bill of Rights? Are we still doing that?" Cam asked.

"Your memory is sharp as a tack. Well done. I thought the alarms at the National Archives would have frazzled your mind," I joked.

Cam looked at me, lifting one eyebrow.

"Just kidding. Yes," I said. "The original plan was to travel back in time to witness the Bill of Rights. But I thought it was important to first meet and get to know James Madison, and learn about the Constitution as a whole. You see, the Bill of Rights is a part of the U.S. Constitution. In fact, it is the first ten additions to the Constitution. They are called amendments, and include the freedom of speech, religion, and press."

"Ah, okay, but I have my eye on you," Cam said, joking. I remembered the fake eye prank he pulled on the class on his first day in school.

Just then a warm gust of wind blew past us. A distant sound of thunder gently rumbled. Out of the corner of my eye, in the distance, I caught a flash of brown. At first, I could not make it out. But when I focused carefully I saw him in the distance, bouncing along.

"Liberty!" I exclaimed. Surprisingly, he heard me and headed back in our direction right away.

"Hey, what about Freedom and her grandpa?" Tommy said, "We have been in history awhile now. Aren't they waiting for us? They are going to freak out when they look and don't know where we are."

"Don't worry," I said. "No matter how long we stay in the past, we will time-jump back to the same time we left. We want to find our answers quickly, though, and not change history."

Seeing the approaching storm and knowing we needed a place to stay for the night, we found rooms at a boardinghouse nearby. Liberty couldn't stay with us indoors, so I broke the news that he had to stay at a local livery. Liberty reluctantly agreed, so long as he was well fed.

The next morning I awoke rested to the sound of a rooster crowing. The goose down mattress, comforter, and pillow made me feel like I was floating on clouds. However, I knew I would have to go outside to use an outhouse, as indoor plumbing was rare in 1787. On a table, beside the bed, sat a ceramic basin to wash my hands and face.

After preparing myself for the day I exited my room and knocked on Cam and Tommy's door. "Good morning, boys. Are you up? Rise and shine. We have a Constitutional Convention to visit." I was anxious to start the day.

As the door opened, Tommy looked refreshed, his blond hair neatly combed. He was smiling widely. "Hi, Mr. Revere. I'm ready, but Cam is moving a little slow this morning."

Tommy opened the door all the way and I could see Cam with his eyes only half open, barely awake. He pushed himself slowly up and sat on the edge of his bed but was slumped over. He yawned, stretched, and then plopped back down on his pillow. "I just need a second," he said. "I didn't sleep much last night 'cause Tommy snores like a horse."

"That wasn't me," Tommy said defensively. "It was Liberty."

Out of nowhere Liberty appeared against a wall with a guilty expression on his face.

I quickly stepped into the room and shut the door behind me. "Liberty," I whispered, loudly, "what are you doing in here?"

"How was I supposed to get any sleep with a snoring horse," Cam complained.

"Sorry," said Liberty. "But I slept like a baby once I got into your room. Sheesh, yesterday was a long day."

So much for Liberty staying at the livery. I should have known!

"I slept great, too," said Tommy. "Then again, my nickname in Cub Scouts was 'Sleeping Bear.'"

Knowing we had little time I said, "Cam, splash some water on your face, get your shoes on, and let's head outside. You boys probably need to visit the outhouse. We'll grab breakfast on the way to the Convention."

"Can I just say I'm really glad I live in the future where we have indoor plumbing?" said Tommy.

"No kidding," Cam said, yawning. "How did people survive without flushing toilets and hot showers?"

"Yes, we are very spoiled in the twenty-first century," I said.

Independence Hall, where the Convention was being held, was only a few blocks from where we slept. As we reached

Chestnut Street the skies of eighteenth-century Philadelphia looked especially gloomy. A slight hot breeze kicked up some litter that blew up and hit me in the face. A young boy carrying a stack of newspapers pushed past us.

"Independence Hall is up ahead," said Liberty. "As your tour guide I'd also like to point out that on this same street is the home of the one and only Dr. Benjamin Franklin—the famous inventor, printer, publisher, and Patriot."

"Awesome," said Tommy. "Maybe we'll see Dr. Franklin at the Convention. This time please don't bring him back to modern day like you did when we first saw him."

"That was a mistake, and I have already apologized for that! It won't happen again for sure," Liberty exclaimed, clomping along on the cobblestones as we walked.

I really hoped we could enter a room called Assembly Hall, where the delegates were meeting.

"Do they have beds at the Convention?" Cam asked. "I seriously need to catch some z's."

I was so busy looking at the ground to avoid potholes that when I looked up I was caught by surprise. Against a cloudy sky, the spire of Independence Hall stood before us.

"Liberty, there's a large tree near the corner of the building. I suggest you wait there. We will be back outside soon. Hopefully, we can get a glimpse of the Convention."

Liberty looked up at the storm clouds. "Okay, but don't take too long. Those are cumulonimbus clouds."

"I haven't seen any lightning, so I'm sure we'll be okay," I said as I reached into his saddlebag and pulled out a special treat I had prepared earlier. "Here," I said. "I cored out the middle of this apple and filled it with a few sugar cubes."

"Yummy," said Liberty, licking his lips. "It's like my very own Tootsie Pop. Hmm, I wonder how many licks it will take me to get to the center?"

Once Liberty was preoccupied with his apple, Cam, Tommy, and I walked up the steps to Independence Hall. I was thrilled. Eleven years before, in 1776, Cam and I visited the same location to witness the signing of the Declaration of Independence. I took a breath and pushed through the large double doors.

There was a crowd milling in front of us. We made our way through and walked down the hallway to the left. I saw a set of two large white doors that looked familiar. I was sure I had seen them before in a famous historic painting. "That must be it, Assembly Hall. The delegates should be inside," I said.

Before I could stop him, Tommy raced over to the doors, but luckily they were locked. We certainly couldn't bolt in and make a huge scene! I had to figure out a plan to get James Madison's attention, without disturbing the debates.

As Cam started to nod off on a nearby bench, Tommy rubbed his hands together and asked, "So what's the plan, Mr. Revere?"

Just then the doors opened and two delegates walked out dressed in dark coats and breeches, similar to mine. One delegate looked at us quickly and then turned back to his fellow delegate as they briskly walked down the hallway.

"Oh man, I recognize that look," said Cam, who was wide awake now and standing next to us. "It's the same look my mom gives when she is really steamed about something."

"Yeah, I wouldn't want to be whoever they are mad at," Tommy added.

"One mom blowing off steam is bad enough. A room full of them, whoa, watch out!" said Cam.

I nodded. "Those men have good reason to be upset. Like Mr. Madison mentioned yesterday, all of the delegates at this Convention are here to represent their state and their people. Each representative and each state has a different idea about how the country should go forward after declaring independence from Great Britain."

I tried to explain. "Have you ever been with your family and everyone agrees they want dinner, but no one can agree on where to go?" I wiped a bead of sweat from my brow.

"Yeah, that happens practically every time we're together," said Tommy. "I always vote for pizza but everybody else likes burgers."

"Well, the same kind of debate is happening here right now, but it is much more serious than where to go for dinner," I said. "Keep in mind they just fought a war for independence. They sacrificed greatly for their freedom. And they're fighting to keep it."

"So why doesn't James Madison or George Washington do what my dad does? He says that if we put up a fuss about where to eat he will make us peanut butter and jelly sandwiches. I mean he throws down the law," Tommy said.

I chuckled. I was impressed at their ability to make such a complex idea understandable.

"Very shrewd, Tommy, but there was so much passion about what the Constitution should be and the how the government should be organized that it wasn't easy for Mr. Madison to tell them to hurry up and decide. But he certainly held his ground," I said.

We heard more raised voices from the Assembly Hall. Curiosity got the best of us so we tiptoed toward the doors.

"I got this," said Cam. One of the delegates forgot to close the door fully on his way out. Cam took advantage of the moment and opened the door a sliver farther so he could peek inside. Cam turned back and mouthed, "Whoa."

"What? What's happening?" asked Tommy.

Before I knew it, both Tommy and Cam were peering through the cracked door watching the debate. All three of us were now crowded at the door, peering in with one eye each. I had to take my tricorner hat off to get close enough.

A Convention delegate was standing up at his table, talking, while everyone else was sitting at little desks facing him.

Cam whispered, "I think I see George Washington and James Madison at the front of the room."

"Cool!" Tommy exclaimed.

Beads of sweat dripped down both sides of my face. It was definitely hot, but I was also nervous. This Convention was top secret. In my history research I read that one delegate got in trouble for leaving his notes out in public, and General Washington lectured everyone about it.

Just then a man came bolting toward the door heading right in our direction. "Someone is coming," I blurted, turning from the door. We scurried away like cats on a hot tin roof.

Tommy and Cam made a beeline for the exit. As I backpedaled I tripped and landed on my backside. Lightning flashed outside and two seconds later, thunder. I scrambled to my feet as quickly as possible. As I tried to get up a familiar voice from behind me said, "Mr. Revere, is that you?" I was shocked to hear someone calling my name. I turned around to see, of all people, George Washington.

"Sir, oh my goodness, General Washington, it is a pleasure to see you again." I was once again starstruck. General George Washington had already won the Revolutionary War and within two years he would be voted the first President of the United States. Unfortunately, I had no idea how I was going to explain our arrival eleven years after we first visited. Luckily, Tommy and Cam, who were the same age as when we last visited, were far enough away that I would not have to explain.

"It is good to see you again," said Washington. "James Madison mentioned you were in town."

Surprisingly, he appeared very calm and collected for having just been in the middle of the highly confrontational debate room. George Washington was the definition of a leader—steady on the surface but likely boiling inside.

"Mr. Revere, you seem as youthful as I remember you last," he said.

"General Washington, I could say the same about you," I replied. He stood straight, but despite my words I noticed he had a tiny stoop in his shoulders. I asked, "How are your horses?"

At this, General Washington smiled. His countenance had a faraway look. "I wish I were with them right now at my home in Mount Vernon," he replied. "But the Articles of Confederation need to be changed so we are here, ensuring the freedom we won in the Revolution is guaranteed today and, hopefully, for generations to come."

The smell of rain wafted through an open hallway window. I hoped the boys weren't getting wet outside. I hoped Liberty wasn't a nervous wreck. And I hoped I was not gawking too much at the exceptional American standing again in front of me.

George Washington put his hand on my shoulder and whispered, "I know you are a true Patriot and we trust you. I would like to invite you into the Assembly Hall to hear a few minutes of the debate. But I must warn you that we must maintain the strictest secrecy. James Madison tells me we are creating a new world."

"I would be most honored," I replied.

"Excellent. The debates will begin again shortly," he said as he reentered the room.

Just then Tommy and Cam came running down the hallway. Breathless, Tommy said, "Mr. Revere, you won't believe what we just saw."

I could hardly contain my joy. "You're telling me! George Washington just invited us to hear the debates. Well, technically, he just invited me, but if you both are quiet you can slip in behind me. Let's go."

As I turned to leave, Cam tugged on my coat and said, "Wait, Mr. Revere. There's something we have to tell you."

"Is Liberty all right?" I asked. "He didn't run away, did he?"

"No, he's still outside, but that's not—" said Tommy before I cut him off.

"We will only be in the Assembly Hall for a few minutes, just enough time to hear some of the debate. This is a once-in-a-lifetime opportunity for us. Come on, we better hurry before they begin again."

My stomach was fluttering as we entered the Assembly Hall. Some delegates looked up but then turned back to their work as we squeezed our way into the back. The room was about forty feet by forty feet, small for fifty-five delegates. Desks were neatly arranged with men at each table and two in front. Everything looked green, and each table had a fountain pen and notes spread around.

The Assembly Room of Independence Hall looked like this in 1787.
Can you imagine what it would be like to hear the delegates
debate the Constitution?

Tommy pointed and whispered, "Oh, oh, there's Mr. Madison."

Madison was seated in an elevated chair at the front of the room near General Washington.

"Wow, he looks really busy up there," added Cam. Bits of sunlight streamed in through small cracks in the closed windows.

Several delegates looked back at us. I whispered to the boys, "We'd better keep our voices down." There was very little space left in the Assembly Hall, so we pushed our backs up against the wall and tried to be inconspicuous.

We listened intently as the delegates gave passionate speeches about freedom and justice and equality. The room seemed to get hotter and hotter. It felt like there was no air at all, as the debates became more intense.

Without any warning, lightning flashed with a thunderous crack.

Tommy looked worried, and I wondered if he was thinking of Liberty outside in the storm.

George Washington stood and called for a short reprieve from the sweltering room.

"Remember this moment, boys. It's important," I said. "A miracle is happening in this room. A government is being created for the people, by the people. These men are debating the very document we use today over two hundred years later. Think about it."

"I've never thought of it like that before," said Cam.

"Me either," said Tommy. "I mean I've seen a copy of the Constitution hanging in my grandfather's house and I knew it was important, but I never really thought about what it means, and how much went into it." He pulled out his grandfather's notebook and made a few notes.

"This might be a good time for us to check on Liberty," I said.

"Good idea!" said both boys, eagerly.

As we headed for the doors a man stood up from the back right table. I paused when I heard him mention "Bill of Rights." He was speaking to several other delegates beside him in a very loud and boisterous voice. As I studied his face I realized this was George Mason.

"We need a Bill of Rights," he repeated in a louder voice.

"Boys, come here," I whispered. "The man speaking over there is George Mason. Mr. Mason is right up there with important Americans like James Madison, George Washington, and Benjamin Franklin."

"Mr. Revere, there sure are a lot of Georges," said Cam. "I mean I guess it's okay as long as they don't have a 'king' in front of their name," he joked.

"True," I nodded. "King George is not going to win any popularity contests in America. But neither is George Mason in this room. After months of negotiations, Mr. Mason is adamant that the Constitution needs a Bill of Rights to protect the rights of the people."

"Wait, I just remembered the Bill of Rights is also hanging on my grandfather's wall," Tommy added. "Right next to the Constitution. Just like in the National Archives building."

"You are right, Tommy," I said. "The Constitution and the Bill of Rights go hand in hand in modern day, but during this Convention the delegates couldn't agree on whether or not adding the Bill of Rights was a good idea."

George Mason continued speaking while most of the delegates shook their heads in protest. You could tell Mr. Mason was getting upset.

This exceptional American is known as
the "Father of the Bill of Rights."
Can you guess who he is? This is George Mason.

"It would give great quiet to the people. We could prepare the bill in a few hours and the rights of the people will be protected," exclaimed George Mason.

Another delegate responded, "There is no need for it. We already have the three branches and representation of the people in Congress, plus a court and a president. The Bill of Rights is an addition we do not need. Let's move on."

"Are you blind? Can you not see what will happen without a bill to protect the people's rights?" shouted Mason.

I could see James Madison at the front of the room, looking over with interest at the heated argument. Benjamin Franklin was sitting nearby with his cane, observing the passionate outburst. George Washington was standing at the front of the room speaking with another delegate.

"It's not that we do not need rights, but we already have rights in the Constitution," another delegate offered and began to walk back to his seat.

"Yes, but we must guarantee these rights to the people," said Mr. Mason. "We must have constitutional protection for individual liberties that are clearly laid out. If not, what will stop the government from taking away the freedoms of our citizens?" George Mason said.

There was a general buzz in the room. The storm outside seemed to have passed and I could hear yammering between delegates as they hashed out their thoughts. Some delegates hunched over their tables with others from their state, whispering.

Finally, the other delegate said, "I hear you, Mr. Mason, but it is very hot in this room and we have been arguing for months. I invite you to present your idea and let us vote on the Bill of

Rights. However, we need the Constitution to protect our freedoms *now*."

"And what exactly will this Bill of Rights include?" asked another delegate.

George Mason paused. He took a deep breath and said, "It will preserve the rights of the people. As we stated in the Virginia Declaration, the people have certain inherent rights, including free speech, press, religion, and trial by jury. The people cannot be deprived of these rights by the government, and they should be included in this Constitution."

I felt a tug on my coat sleeve. It was Tommy. He whispered, "My grandfather always says that freedom of speech is really important. He talks about how lucky we are to live in a country where we can think and say what we want without being killed or put in jail like in other countries. I never knew it was the Bill of Rights that gave us that freedom."

Cam added, "I bet George Mason will be happy once they vote yes on the Bill of Rights."

"Actually, the Bill of Rights was voted down at first," I whispered. "Meaning the delegates did not agree with George Mason. He was so angry about it, in fact, he refused to sign the Constitution."

There was another rumble of thunder outside. Cam said, "I really think we better go check on Liberty."

Tommy whispered something to Cam as we walked toward the doors leading to the hallway.

"Keeping secrets from me, Tommy?" I asked, teasing.

"It probably won't be a secret for long," he replied.

"Tommy, whatever it is I doubt it would surprise me."

As we opened the door to meet up with Liberty, I couldn't believe my eyes.

Liberty was standing at the bottom of the stairs in front of a parked carriage. He was wearing what looked to be a tall checkered hat. As we got closer, I realized he was actually harnessed to the carriage and was fully drenched in rainwater.

"Liberty!" I exclaimed. I rushed to the bottom of the stairs and whispered, "Are you trying out for a horse-and-carriage ride in Central Park?"

Liberty looked both ways to make sure we were alone before replying. He protested, "This is humiliating, Revere, very humiliating. I am not a fan, I am not in favor."

Trying not to laugh, I asked, "How come you guys didn't tell me?"

"We tried!" Tommy and Cam said in unison.

"I thought being tied to a tree was bad. This is downright insulting. I mean really, it is not good for my mojo to be strapped to a carriage. Puleeese! This is something Little Liberty would do happily, but not me," Liberty said, shaking water from his back.

"You know you would be a great horse-and-buggy show in a Fourth of July parade," Cam joked.

"Okay, okay, in all seriousness, how on earth did you get strapped to the carriage?" I whispered.

"Well, this man must have thought I was his horse and pulled me over here while I was in a deep sleep. I was dreaming of a field of crunchy carrots, and before I realized what was happening I had this ridiculous hat on my head!" Liberty replied. "And I was strapped in, so I couldn't disappear. Just look at me, I'm a tourist attraction."

I spent a few minutes figuring out how to unleash Liberty's bridle and set him free from the humiliation. Once I got the final strap undone, Liberty sprinted down the street like he was after the last carrot ice-cream cone on the planet.

"We should get back to modern day before the owner of this buggy gets back," I said. "We also have to find Freedom and her grandfather."

We caught up with Liberty a few hundred yards away in a secluded spot.

"Are we safe? Are the cops after us? Is my mug shot up on all the buildings?" Liberty said, shaking.

"The best thing we can do now is get back to modern day," I replied as the boys hoisted themselves up onto Liberty's saddle.

"You got it, Captain. Rush, rush, rushing from history!" Liberty shouted with gusto and the colorful time portal appeared.

This statue currently stands across from Independence Hall in Philadelphia, Pennsylvania. It represents the signers of the Constitution.
Behind the statue is the former home of Gilbert Stuart, who painted the George Washington portrait saved by Dolley Madison.

Chapter 7

*T*ogether, *we leapt* into the time portal back to modern day and instantly found ourselves where we had started. Tommy looked through Liberty's saddlebag and found his football. He grabbed it and threw it to Cam, who caught it over his shoulder. I looked at my watch and was relieved to see that Liberty had timed it perfectly.

"Great job, Liberty. We're back at the National Archives building," I said, patting him on his side.

"Am I good or am I good? Cam, put that in the 'Liberty is Amazing' file," Liberty bragged as he tried to high-hoof each of us.

"I thought you usually deposited those in the compliment bank," Tommy said, laughing.

"Valid point, Tommy, but on this occasion I thought filing was in order," Liberty said with a grin.

As we approached the front of the building there was no

sign of Freedom or her grandpa. I texted Freedom's grandfather and let him know we were available to meet when and where convenient. He texted back and suggested the Lincoln Memorial on the National Mall in half an hour.

"Are you guys up for another walk?" I asked.

"Sure, but can we grab a snack somewhere?" Tommy replied.

Liberty looked over my shoulder and said, "Are you looking for a place to eat? Because I'm with Tommy, and could use something yummy for my tummy, if you know what I'm saying."

I gave Liberty a few apples from his saddlebag to tide him over and said, "Let's get some warm nuts from that street cart."

We bought several packs for the mile-long walk down the National Mall. As we walked, several American flags caught my eye. An older woman passed us wearing a prominent flag on her T-shirt with a saying that read *America the Beautiful*.

As we approached the Lincoln Memorial, Cam shouted, "Freedom, over here!" and waved to Freedom who was about thirty yards away. He liked to play tough on the outside but was one of the most caring young men I had ever met.

"Hi, guys," Freedom said, running over to us. "Wow, those alarms were really scary!"

Both boys looked at each other and then at me and said, "Yeahhhh," in unison.

"I'm glad all is okay at the National Archives. I kept checking the news on my phone and they reported there was a disturbance but didn't go into detail. Finally, an employee spoke to the media and said all was clear," Freedom's grandfather said.

"Whewwww, lucky for us," Tommy said, under his breath.

Liberty made a fake coughing sound to get everyone's attention and said, "Soooooooo, does anyone have any answers for me? Did anyone solve the clue?"

"Oh gosh. Thank you, Liberty, I mean Commander. I almost forgot I did," Freedom said. "Here is my written answer. Can I still get my point?" She handed her sketchpad to Liberty.

Liberty's deep voice returned and he said, "Yes, Special Agent, point to you. Cam won a point at Union Station, Tommy won a point at the Washington Monument, and Freedom just got her point from the National Archives. That means that all agents are currently tied with one point each."

Freedom's grandfather smiled and walked away for a second to take a cell phone call.

"I hear from Liberty you guys were up to no good, I mean yo-yo no good," Freedom joked.

"Very funny, I was trying to do a cool trick, but . . ." Tommy started to say but his voice trailed off.

Freedom smiled, shook her head, and said, "Hey, you guys didn't time-travel without me, did you?" She eyed us suspiciously. She could probably smell the eighteenth-century sewer lingering on our clothes.

"Um," Cam replied, "we better tell you later."

"Mr. Revere!" Freedom exclaimed.

"I owe you one, Freedom," I said. "I will remember to take you to a great spot."

Freedom's grandfather returned from his phone call and gave Freedom a loving hug.

We walked to the front of the Lincoln Memorial and I asked everyone to gather around. I said, "This is a very important spot that we are standing in. This is the location where Martin Luther King, Jr., gave his 'I Have a Dream' speech in 1963."

Years ago I memorized his words and they wafted through my mind as I looked out from the spot where he spoke the words to hundreds of thousands of marchers.

In a sense we've come to our nation's capital to cash a check. When the architects of our republic wrote the magnificent words of the Constitution and the Declaration of Independence, they were signing a promissory note to which every American was to fall heir.

I added, "Martin Luther King was speaking about the men we met in Philadelphia in 1787. The architects of the republic included Washington and Madison, Franklin and Mason, and all the delegates we watched in person debate the future of our country."

Cam added, "He was talking about *all men created equal,* right? Like in the Declaration of Independence."

"Yes, that's right, Cam. And that although slavery was over, in the 1960s people were still fighting for equal rights, under the Thirteenth, Fourteenth, and Fifteenth Amendments to the Constitution," I said. I felt that these concepts were probably over their heads right now, but I wanted them to hear about it for their future studies.

Tommy opened his notebook and starting writing. Freedom's grandfather walked over and put his arm around Tommy. "You doing okay?" he asked.

Tommy shrugged and looked up. "Doing good," he replied, but his face dropped into a frown.

Freedom's grandfather looked back to the group and said, "We will talk more about the issues that faced and are facing our country as we go. It is important for you kids to keep asking

questions as you learn. That is the most important part of study-ing history. Remember the statue with the seeds?"

The Crew nodded.

We stayed as long as we could at the Lincoln Memorial, but I realized the day was quickly passing and we still had to get to our next destination before it closed to the public.

As we walked, my mind drifted to the first time I met Lib-erty. Back then I never imagined I would be able to travel back in time to visit the Founders of our nation and see them craft the words that became a symbol to the people of America and around the world. I felt goose bumps run up my arms as I pondered all that this country has been blessed with. Yes, we are not perfect, I thought, but we are Americans, and I am so proud.

"Where are we going now, Mr. Revere?" Tommy asked.

"The next building were are going to visit is also an American landmark," I replied. "In fact, it is one of the greatest symbols of freedom in the United States." I pointed to the Capitol Building on the map and showed everyone the route.

"The U.S. Capitol Building is located on the northeast side of the National Mall," I said.

We kept walking until the shining Capitol Building came into focus in the distance. The giant round dome at the top of the building was bright against the blue sky. Three American flags waved on top of the building, in the middle and on both sides.

"Wow," said Freedom, following my gaze. "That is really cool. Every building here looks like a piece of art."

"If there's time, you should draw the National Mall or the Capitol Building. I bet it would be really cool," Tommy said.

Freedom smiled broadly, as did her grandfather.

"Thank you, I can't wait," Freedom replied.

"Hey, Tommy, I hear you throw a pretty good spiral," Freedom's grandfather said, shifting his attention to Tommy.

"Aww, thanks. I mean it's okay. But I try to practice a lot. My grandfather told me if I keep practicing I will get better and better," Tommy replied.

"Well, come on, let's walk over here out of the way and you can throw me the ball," Freedom's grandfather said, motioning for Tommy to follow him. I watched from a distance.

"All right, fire away," Freedom's grandfather said as he backed up to receive the ball.

Tommy leaned back and threw the ball into the air, the spiral holding tightly as it traveled. Freedom's grandfather caught the ball in both hands and smiled widely.

"Well done, Tommy! That looked perfect to me."

Tommy's face lit up with the compliment and he said, "Thank you! Maybe we can practice some more later."

After about ten minutes we reached the steps of the Capitol and stopped for a moment to fully absorb the surroundings. We craned our necks up to look at the architectural masterpiece. Near the Capitol steps, with the white stone proudly rising above us, things were almost quiet, except for a few distant car horns. I imagined senators and representatives walking up the steps discussing a bill or another national event.

"Hey, I can see a statue at the top of the dome," said Cam.

"That is the Statue of Freedom," I replied.

"But if we were at the Emerald City it would be a statue of the Wizard of Oz," said Liberty, obviously in his own world.

I clarified: "Before arriving I did a little research. The Statue of Freedom stands nineteen feet and six inches tall."

Tommy looked at Freedom and said jokingly, "First the Charters of Freedom and now a Statue of Freedom? You're like the most popular person in Washington, D.C."

"As long as you don't cast me in bronze and attach me to the top of a tall building we can still be friends," teased Freedom.

Her grandfather added, "And believe it or not the Statue of Freedom weighs fifteen thousand pounds."

"Freedom weighs fifteen thousand pounds," said Liberty, "Wow, I would not have guessed that."

Tommy and Cam burst out laughing.

"Not me," explained Freedom, a little embarrassed. "He's referring to the statue."

"Ohhhhhhh," said Liberty. "For a second I thought I was as strong as the Hulk. I mean, I do carry you when we jump through the portal."

"Mr. Revere," Cam asked, "you mean a hundred and fifty pounds, right?"

I checked the info on my phone and replied, "No, the official Capitol website says the Statue of Freedom is made of bronze and weighs fifteen thousand pounds. That's heavier than several elephants."

"It just shows you how massive and strong the building is to hold a statue that heavy," said Freedom's grandfather.

I looked up at the two sets of huge steps heading up to the Capitol entrance. Birds chirped in large green trees that were a contrast to the white background. We were now closer to the American flags flying above the Capitol and I knew they indicated whether Congress was in session.

The United States Congress meets here at the U.S. Capitol
to debate important laws much as the Founding Fathers did in 1787.

I kept reading aloud from my phone: "It took nine million pounds of ironwork to create the dome. It also says that the Statue of Freedom is a female figure with long, flowing hair wearing a helmet with an eagle's head and feathers. In her left hand she holds the shield of the United States with thirteen stripes."

I covered my phone a bit from the glaring sun, then continued reading. "Let's see, it says that on her pedestal is a globe with the motto—*E Pluribus Unum*, which means, 'Out of many, one.'"

"What does 'out of many, one' even mean, Mr. Revere?" asked Cam.

"It means that out of the many colonies or states, we formed one united country," I replied.

"That makes sense," said Tommy. "The Constitutional Convention was all about *E Pluribus Unum*, right Mr. Revere? James Madison wanted to form one united country. And the Constitution makes us *E Pluribus Unum*—out of many, one, or several states that form one country."

"He may be goofy, but he's a smart goofy," said Cam, patting Tommy's head like a puppy dog.

"Commander, what about the next clue in our mission?" Freedom asked. "It says on our cards we will receive our next clue at the U.S. Capitol Building." Cam and Tommy pulled out their cards.

"Sharp thinking, Agent Freedom, you are on a roll," Liberty's low voice returned.

Liberty puckered his lips and made the sound of a trumpet—the kind you hear at the beginning of a grand event or ceremony. When he finished he cleared his throat and said, "Lady and gentlemen! On your marks, get set . . . oh wait, we aren't running anywhere, scratch that, this is a mission clue." Liberty was never short of antics. "Captain, please pass the map."

I pulled a piece of paper that looked like a faded treasure map from his saddlebag, and Liberty read it aloud in a deep voice.

> Go to the area inside the Capitol with the huge dome and lots of paintings on the walls. There you will find a statue of an exceptional American we have already met. 1. What is his name? 2. What state is written on the base of the statue? 3. What is in his right hand and what is in his left hand?

Cam, Tommy, and Freedom all read the clue in detail and I put it in my pocket for future reference.

Liberty added, "Make sure to text your answers to Captain Revere from the place where you found the statue. The first with a correct answer receives the mission point."

"I called ahead and asked if there was someone who could give my incredibly well-behaved students a tour," I said, raising my eyebrows and smiling at Cam and Tommy. "I especially want to emphasize the words *incredibly well-behaved*."

Cam replied, "I can't speak for Tommy, Mr. Revere. But you won't get any pranks from me. Do you think we should put Tommy in a straitjacket?"

"Ha, ha," said Tommy.

I turned to Liberty and repeated, "*Well-behaved*, got it?"

"What are you looking at me for?" asked Liberty.

"Oh, I don't know," I said, casually. "Maybe because horses are not allowed inside the Capitol Building, so you will need to stay outside. And before you even think about turning invisible and sneaking inside, don't, because it'll be crowded and someone is bound to bump into you."

"I can be well-behaved outside, too," Liberty harrumphed.

"Even when you are left unsupervised?" I asked.

Liberty looked over my shoulder and exclaimed, "Would you look at that dome?"

He was a master at avoiding questions when he wanted to.

After distracting everyone Liberty continued: "Sorry, I can't take credit for the dome or the awesome statue on top of the Capitol Building. But I can take credit for this." Suddenly Liberty burped so loud and so long it caused several tourists to look in our direction.

You would have thought the Crew had just heard the funniest joke on the planet. Even Freedom's grandpa was laughing.

"Did you not just tell me you could be well-behaved?" I scolded, softly.

"Sorry," said Liberty, apologetically. "But on the bright side I'm pretty sure that was a new record. Tommy and I were having a burping contest the other day so when I felt that one coming on I just had to try to beat Tommy's record. Oh, and technically, I said I could be well-behaved when I'm unsupervised."

I shrugged and shook my head. "Okay," I said. "Let's find the entrance to the visitors center and find our tour guide."

"Have fun storming the castle," Liberty said. "And don't worry about me. I'll just be out here swatting flies with my tail. But I am not jealous. Nope, not at all."

"Don't worry," said Freedom patting Liberty's neck. "I will tell you everything as we go. We can communicate mind to mind, remember? We'll send each other updates so you don't miss out on anything."

"Why didn't I think of that?" said Liberty. "Okay, sounds like a plan. I won't even know you're gone."

Freedom led Liberty to a shady tree, fed him a few treats from his saddlebag, and then returned to the group.

"Thank you, Freedom," I said. "I'm so glad you're with us on this field trip."

"Me, too," said Freedom, smiling. "Just don't go anywhere without me."

It didn't take us long to find the visitor entryway beneath the East Plaza of the Capitol Building. We walked downstairs and passed through security.

"No more yo-yo-type incidents okay?" I said looking at Cam and Tommy.

They both sheepishly grinned.

In the visitors center, we saw a large plaster model of the Freedom statue we saw on top of the Capitol dome. A large statue of King Kamehameha of Hawaii also fascinated the Crew. After a quick walk around, we entered the line for the tour and made our way to the front.

A greeter warmly welcomed us and gave us our individual tour passes. She said, "Welcome to the United States Capitol Building," and motioned for us to continue ahead. We watched a short introductory movie and then made our way to the Capitol Rotunda.

Freedom whispered, "Don't forget we have to find the answers to Commander Liberty's clue."

We walked into the Rotunda and were mesmerized by its beauty. It was truly astonishing. I did a 360 and got dizzy looking at all the amazing sights. There were intricate carvings on the walls and a gold ceiling. The floors sparkled and the flat columns rose in a circle. All around us, tourists admired the sheer magnitude of the room.

"Ah, I got this!" Cam exclaimed, pointing to large paintings on the ground floor. "Those look like the paintings Liberty was talking about. The statue has to be around here somewhere."

Freedom's grandfather looked carefully and said out loud, "I think Cam is right. There are the Pilgrims on the *Speedwell* and the signing of the Declaration of Independence."

"Grandpa!" Freedom exclaimed. "Whose team are you on?"

Cam's eyes darted from one side of the room to the other, but he did not seem to find what he was looking for.

"Whoa, my bedroom ceiling sure doesn't look like this," said Tommy, reverently.

"So where's our tour guide?" asked Cam, searching the room.

Freedom tapped my back and whispered, "Hey, Mr. Revere, I think you have a twin." Her eyes darted to someone over my shoulder.

"Good day. I couldn't help but notice your great taste in clothing," said someone from behind me. I turned to see a man wearing a colonial outfit similar to mine, including a tricornered hat, vest, breeches, stockings, and boots—straight from the 1700s. His name badge said BENJAMEER, U.S. CAPITOL BUILDING TOUR GUIDE. Benjameer smiled and said, "I could not have chosen a better set of breeches myself." He wore white gloves and turned to us with a bow.

"Why, thank you, sir," I said, hesitatingly. I noticed the other tour guides wore red blazers, but Benjameer wore what appeared to be a brown authentic colonial jacket. And he acted as if he were literally from the eighteenth century. We were in a big city, though, and I thought this guy could be a little on the crazy side. Then again, he was wearing a tour guide name badge.

The man turned to the rest of our group and said, "My name is Benjameer Franklot. It is a pleasure to meet you." He bowed deeply and said, "I was told that a Mr. Rush Revere would be here at about this time with some well-behaved students." He eyed all of us carefully.

"Oh, good, yes, I'm Rush Revere. And these are my history students."

"Wonderful," Benjameer declared. "I'm honored to be your tour guide. Feel free to take pictures but do not under any circumstance touch anything. Does everyone understand?"

We all nodded.

Tommy raised his hand.

"Oh, I see we already have a question. Good, excellent. I'm sure that this Capitol Rotunda has spawned great curiosity. Go ahead, lad, I can tell you are wise beyond your years and have a question that will stimulate all our minds."

I shouldn't have been too surprised when Tommy asked, "Is Benjameer Franklot your real name? It sounds like you could be the evil twin of Benjamin Franklin."

Cam let out a stifled laugh.

I took a deep breath and exhaled slowly.

Our tour guide gave an annoyed smile and replied, "Benjameer Franklot is a perfectly fine name. And, no, I'm not the evil twin of Benjamin Franklin. However, asking questions, as ridiculous as they may be, is your given right as an American citizen." He sniffed and rolled his neck before exclaiming,

"Before we begin, can anyone tell me what the Capitol Building represents?"

Cam looked at Freedom and back at me. "Does it represent Freedom?" he asked, seemingly unsure of the answer.

"Yes, young man, it does," Benjameer said, warming to the group. "The United States Capitol Building is an American symbol of freedom. As you may have learned in your history class, the United States has three branches of government. The Capitol is part of the legislative branch. The laws of the entire country are made right here within the House of Representatives and Senate chambers."

Tommy and Cam grinned and looked at each other with a twinkle in their eyes. Freedom looked at them sideways.

"James Madison told us about all three branches of government and how they came to be in the United States Constitution," Tommy said.

Benjameer looked puzzled and uncertain if Tommy was pulling his leg, again. Freedom's grandfather also looked at us quizzically.

"Let's move ahead to Statuary Hall, which is right down this way," Benjameer said.

"Hold on a second, Benjameer," Tommy said, suppressing a laugh. The class clown was coming out in full force now. "We are here on a top-secret mission, and need to get to the bottom of something."

"Indeed, I am *sure* you are," Benjameer said, dismissively.

"Really we are," added Cam. "We need to find a statue of somebody we've already met."

Benjameer laughed. "Unless you have a time machine in your

pocket I highly doubt there is a statue of anyone *you* have met here," Benjameer said, turning to go. "The only statues here are . . ." He began to point to statues around the room, naming each statue. ". . . and, of course, George Washington."

"Whoa, whoa, wait a second Mr. Franklot," Tommy said, looking at the Crew, "That's our man, G Dub." I looked at him with a sideward glance. Instantly, the Crew went running toward the statue of George Washington, leaving Benjameer in a flutter. He was waving his hands up and down. I smiled sympathetically at him and followed.

When Freedom's grandfather and I caught up, I pulled the clue from my pocket and read it out loud to refresh their memory.

"Easy peasy, I got it!" Cam said, typing the answers.

Tommy and Freedom did the same, looking up at each other every once in a while to see who was in the lead like swimmers in an Olympic pool.

My phone beeped three times. Cam's answer came first—*GEORGE WASHINGTON, VIRGINIA.*

Freedom's grandfather nodded at me and said, "Nothing like a little friendly competition to get the minds working."

"The next part of the clue asks what is in his left and right hands," Tommy said, reading from the old parchment.

"It's a sword in his right hand," Cam replied, "but I'm not sure what he's leaning on with his left hand. It looks like a tall barrel or something."

"*That* is a symbol of his civilian life," Benjameer said, having made his way over. "It is a plow, such as one found on his farm at Mount Vernon. The sword in his right hand symbolizes his life in the military and the plow symbolizes his leaving office to go back to civilian life. It represents his love of the country, to retire from office and not become a dictator."

Benjameer raised his hand and curled his fingers like an actor onstage.

"Wow," Tommy said, "that is pretty cool."

The Crew began typing into their phones again—*SWORD*—*PLOW.*

I looked down at my phone and found that Cam again had replied first, if only by a few seconds.

"Could we now please go to the next section of our tour?" Benjameer asked impatiently. Obediently, we followed him toward Statuary Hall.

After a short walk we arrived. Inside the hall were beautifully carved bronze and marble statues. Like the Rotunda, the floors sparkled and everything seemed perfectly constructed. Columns rose around us.

"Statues kind of scare me," Freedom said, reaching out for her grandfather's hand. "Seriously, does anyone else feel like they're being watched?"

Without stopping, Benjameer spoke loudly over his shoulder. "The statues you see were donated by each of the fifty states—two per state—to honor the prominent and notable people." Suddenly, Benjameer stopped at a white marble statue and said, "This is the statue of—"

"It's Samuel Adams," Tommy blurted out, "and it totally looks like him." The statue's arms were folded and he looked as stoic and determined as ever. He even looked a little grumpy with one leg off to the side and his coat hanging down beside him. On the base of the statute it read MASSACHUSETTS.

Tommy continued: "I remember when Samuel Adams showed us the painting of the Boston Massacre. He printed it at Paul Revere's place and then posted it all over town to try to get all the Patriots pumped up about fighting back against the British troops. That guy was one smart thinker."

Benjameer's mouth was still open. You could tell he was trying to make sense of Tommy's personal connection with a man who lived more than two hundred years ago.

Finally, Benjameer said, "Well, technically, yes, that's true." He looked at me with a rather confused look. "Um, let's continue our tour," he said.

We walked down the south wing of the Capitol Building and eventually reached the upper level. "Have any of you seen this room before? Perhaps in photos, or during a State of the Union address by the President, or on C-SPAN?" Benjameer asked, motioning his hand from left to right showcasing the room.

"Um, C-SPAN?" Cam made a funny expression with his face as if to say C-SPAN wasn't on his favorites list.

Below we could see brown desks and comfortable armchairs arranged in a semicircle on tiered platforms. A large American flag hung behind the speaker's podium.

Benjameer stopped, turned, and straightened his coat. His voice echoed as he said, "The United States Capitol Building is the home of two very important chambers. This is the House of Representatives chamber, which is on the south wing. As you can see by the seats below you, there is enough room for hundreds of representatives from Florida to Alaska. They debate the laws of the land right here."

Tommy leaned over and asked, "Wouldn't Mr. Madison

think it was really cool if we went and told him we got to see the two chambers he talked about over dinner? It makes total sense now."

Cam raised his hand and asked, "So where is the other chamber if there are two in the legislative branch?"

"Great question, Cam," Freedom's grandfather said, patting Cam on the back.

Their inquisitive minds never ceased to impress me.

Benjameer responded, "The House of Representatives convenes in the south wing and the United States Senate convenes in the north wing of the Capitol Building. These make up the two chambers of the United States Congress."

I prompted, "In the United States Senate, each state is represented by two senators, elected by the people, regardless of population, correct?"

Benjameer replied, "Yes, indeed, sir, you are correct. This dates back to the Connecticut Compromise, which came about during the drafting of the Constitution in 1787. The people of each state elect two senators who serve six-year terms."

"Yes, we were there! James Madison told us all about the Connecticut Compromise and how he had to give up some of his ideas in the Virginia Plan to get it approved," Tommy said enthusiastically.

Benjameer looked at Tommy with a confused look. Freedom's grandfather gave me a wink.

Breaking the silence, Freedom piped in: "Mr. Revere and his horse, Liberty, are the best history teachers in the world."

"Horse?" Benjameer asked. Everyone looked away with no reply.

This is a photo of the 111th United States Senate,
meeting in the U.S. Capitol Building. There are two senators per state.
The other part of Congress is the House of Representatives.

Just then, Freedom tapped my shoulder and whispered, "Mr. Revere, we have sort of an emergency outside."

Oh no, I thought. What has Liberty gotten himself into this time?

"Liberty told me to tell you that he was minding his own business in front of the building where we left him but it sounds like the Capitol Police didn't want a stray horse wandering the National Mall. So Liberty had to make a break for it."

"He's running from the police?" I asked.

"Yes, but he said not to worry," Freedom clarified. "He's going to give them the slip."

I leaned closer to her and asked, "You mean he's going to turn invisible so the police cannot find him?"

Freedom paused as she reached out to Liberty's mind for more information. "Uh, not exactly," Freedom said. "Apparently, Liberty keeps banana peels in his saddlebag just in case he's being chased. He's literally going to give the police *the slip* by tossing banana peels at them. He says it works when he plays Mario Kart."

By now, the boys were listening to our conversation and were laughing.

"Is something funny?" asked Benjameer with a bit of irritation in his voice.

"I'm so sorry, Mr. Franklot, but we're going to have to end our tour of the Capitol," I said. "We have a friend who needs our help."

"Yeah, we might have to bail him out of jail," whispered Tommy with a smirk.

Chapter 8

As we left the Capitol building to rescue Liberty, Freedom said, "Liberty says he's going to meet us at the northeast corner of the Capitol near Constitution Avenue."

We began to walk that way and Tommy pointed out a banana peel on the sidewalk. "We must be headed in the right direction," he said.

"Liberty's been watching too much TV," said Cam. "Slipping on a banana peel is bogus. It only works in cartoons."

"Whatever," said Tommy. "You'd slip on one, too, just like you and Freedom are going to slip into last place when I'm first to find our next clue!"

As the kids teased each other I searched ahead for any sign of a fugitive horse. After a few minutes we arrived at our rendezvous point.

"Where is he?" asked Cam. "Isn't Liberty supposed to be here?"

Liberty appeared out of nowhere. He was breathing hard and clearly paranoid about being caught.

"I think you're safe," I said. "Nobody's chasing you."

"Whew!" Liberty replied. "You are lucky I wasn't horsenapped, although a nap sounds pretty good right now. But seriously, I was standing where you left me, daydreaming that the Washington Monument was a giant carrot sticking out of the ground, when suddenly I looked up and saw the Capitol Police sneaking up on me. They were close enough to spit gum at."

"Please tell me you didn't spit gum into their hair like you did to that British Redcoat in 1765," I said.

"Of course not," Liberty replied. "The Capitol Police are the good guys. Except when they think I'm a criminal fugitive horse. As soon as I saw them stalking me I backed away slowly. But then they started walking a little faster, so I backed away a little faster, and before I knew it the chase was on. And let me tell you, it's not easy running backward with four legs!"

"Why didn't you just turn invisible?" asked Tommy.

"Not when they're staring directly at me in broad daylight," Liberty said. "Remember, I don't technically turn invisible. I can only blend into my surroundings like a chameleon."

Freedom giggled and said, "You're never invisible to me."

"But you're safe now," I said. "If we bump into the police we'll just tell them we found our lost horse and all is well."

Liberty's breathing calmed and he said, "Lucky for you I can multitask with the best of them. You think I'm only running from the law, but really I'm preparing the next mission clue for the secret agents."

"Bravo, my friend, you are a gentleman and a scholar," I said, knowing Liberty would beam. "But before you jump into the next clue, we are going to have to head to the hotel to grab dinner and tuck in for the night. We want to make sure we are well rested for our big day tomorrow."

We took the Metro to the hotel, and Liberty found his way back to his outdoor bed.

The next morning everyone looked rested when we met Liberty at the park where he slept.

"Oh, oh, can I give the clue now?" Liberty said, almost jumping from one leg to the other.

"Yes, but before you do, I have a few questions of my own to see who was paying attention yesterday," I said. Liberty's shoulders sank.

"Mr. Revere, it sounds like you're giving us a test," Cam said accusingly.

"Not a test," I replied. "Think of it more as I'm pitching you some questions to see if you can hit them."

"Okay, great, then I'm going to hit a grand slam," Tommy said.

"I can't wait to see it," I replied. "Now, who can tell me what we saw so far on our tour of Washington, D.C.?"

"Besides security guards and angry police on horseback, right?" Cam said, laughing. "Just joking; we saw the National Archives, of course."

Freedom nodded and added, "Yes, where some of our country's really important documents are kept, like the Constitution."

"Exactly right, you *were* paying attention," I said, then smiled and glanced at Freedom's grandfather. He looked on proudly.

Tommy raised his hand and said, "We also saw the Capitol Building, where all our country's laws are debated."

"And we saw the Washington Monument," Freedom said, with confidence.

"Wow guys, *fantastico, complimenti, magnifique, parabens*," Liberty said, attempting all accents.

"So, what have we not seen yet?" I asked.

Everyone looked at me blankly.

"Oh, I get what you're doing here, Revere," Liberty said. He was squinting. "Mind if I step in?"

I motioned for Liberty to go ahead.

"Well, James Madison taught us that there are three branches of government in the United States. These were established in the Constitution," Liberty said, professorially. "So far we've seen the Capitol Building, which is part of the legislative branch. So that just leaves two to see." He nodded to his students.

"Wow, Liberty, I'm impressed. I thought it was just fun and games with you," I said. "Sometimes you sail to a random thought but this time you are spot-on."

I patted Liberty's side and pulled out a spear of broccoli from his saddlebag.

Freedom's grandfather took Liberty's lead and added, "If Liberty were arrested, where would he have to go to say he is innocent?"

"Court," Cam said quickly. "And I'm not talking about a basketball court. Although it would be kind of cool to play a game of one-on-one against a judge to defend your innocence."

"Unless the judge is LeBron James," Tommy replied.

"Uh, good point," Cam nodded.

"I'm sure Cam's referring to a court of law," Freedom's grandfather said.

"Exactly right," I said. "Our next stop is the highest court in the United States, called the Supreme Court."

Liberty made an exaggerated coughing sound, to gather everyone's attention. Then he said in a low voice, "Secret agents, the time is now. I am prepared to deliver your next clue. Are you ready?"

The Crew nodded in anticipation and Freedom checked the next number on her mission notecard.

"This is your next clue," Liberty said, dramatically.

> *How many judges are there on the Supreme Court, what are they called, and which branch of government do they serve in?*

Cam said, "Game on!" and started to pull out his phone.

"Ah, ah, ah," Liberty warned. "You must text the answers to Captain Revere from the location where the Supreme Court judges sit when court is in session. That is your mission!"

"Got it," Freedom said, and wrote the clue down in her sketchbook.

"Don't forget our special surprise, Liberty," I reminded him.

"Oh yes, thank you, Captain. If you all do well in this part of the mission, you will receive a special prize," Liberty said. "I will announce it after you *all* correctly complete the Supreme Court objective."

"Cool!" Tommy said.

"We will meet you outside the Supreme Court after we come out, Liberty," I said.

We left the park and took the Metro to a stop near the Supreme Court building. After a short walk we saw the dome of the Capitol Building on our right. To get our bearings I took a quick look around. I could not see past the Capitol dome, but knew that the National Mall behind it stretched all the way down to the Lincoln Memorial.

Lawyers argue cases here at the Supreme Court of the United States.
Above the pillars are the words *Equal Justice Under Law*.

Then I saw it. The Supreme Court of the United States. We walked closer until we were standing in front of it. I had seen movies of people walking up the long set of steps to the court, but somehow everything looked brighter in person. I counted eight giant columns leading up to a triangular top. They looked strong and sturdy and above them, the words EQUAL JUSTICE UNDER LAW.

"Picture time, guys!" Freedom said as we gathered to capture the moment and check another task off the mission list. Behind us flew large American flags.

We made our way to a side entrance and through security.

The inside of the Supreme Court was as awe-inspiring as the Capitol Building. I could have stayed for hours looking at the columns, art, chandeliers, and statues of former justices of the Supreme Court.

"Hey, what is a justice?" Cam asked, looking at an inscription near a statue. "Is it like the Justice League? You know, with Superman, Batman, and Wonder Woman?"

"Not quite," I said. "A justice is a judge who sits on the bench of the Supreme Court. The Supreme Court is the highest court in the land, so a justice is the top judge. There are a total of nine justices on the Supreme Court, and they serve for life, unlike Congress or the President."

"Oh, that's cool!" Tommy said. "I've seen pictures of the justices dressed in black robes sitting next to each other. I didn't really know what they did, though."

"Maybe underneath those robes they're wearing superhero costumes," suggested Cam, smiling.

"The nine justices are extremely cool," Freedom's grandfather said. "They may not be superheroes but they are super at studying

These are the nine justices of the Supreme Court of the United States.
They serve for life and are appointed by the president of the United States.
Can you name them?

the U.S. Constitution. They make sure laws created by Congress protect the rights of the people. Sometimes, the Supreme Court justices will say a law is not 'constitutional.' When they do, they strike it down, and it is no longer the law of the land."

The Crew nodded.

Tommy looked like a lightbulb went off in his head and he began to text.

I looked over his shoulder and read *TO MR. REVERE: NINE JUSTIC—*

Before he could finish, Freedom interrupted and said, "Don't forget you have to text from where the judges sit."

Tommy put his phone down and said, "Thanks, Freedom, good call."

Cam gave a half smile and said, "My mom's the Supreme Court in our house. One time I made a new law that I shouldn't have to wash the dishes. Oh, boy, she struck that faster than a cat falling upside down."

We all laughed along with Cam.

Freedom tugged my shirt and said, "Mr. Revere, could I sketch a little bit in here? It is really pretty."

Just then, Freedom noticed a young girl, with sandy hair and a mouth full of braces, drawing in a notebook. She was sitting by herself on a small bench, seemingly content in her own world.

"Mr. Revere, that girl likes to draw, too. I wonder if she is drawing something for her class about the Supreme Court?" Freedom asked.

"Would you like to go and say hello?"

Freedom smiled and said, "Sure," and began walking toward her. I was surprised at her eagerness to meet a new friend.

"Hi, I'm Freedom," she said in a soft voice. "I really like to draw, too."

The girl, who looked about Freedom's age, looked up.

"What's your name?" Freedom asked.

"My name is Maddie," the girl said quietly. "I love to draw people and places and animals, but only sometimes."

"Me, too," Freedom said, looking down at her notebook. "My teacher said I should draw places in Washington, D.C., so I could remember our field trip."

"Who is your teacher?" Maddie asked. "Is it your mom?"

"No, his name is Mr. Revere. He is our substitute history teacher," Freedom replied, waving me over.

"Cool!" said Maddie. "It's just my mom and me. She's right over there by the courtroom."

I greeted Maddie and stood back a bit to let them talk.

A little way behind me a voice said, "Sorry for intruding. Let's go, Maddie Margaret. We don't want to bother these nice people."

A woman in jeans and a bright blouse ushered Maddie out of her seat.

"It is no bother whatsoever," I said. "We were just complimenting your daughter on her impressive artwork."

Maddie's mother said, "Thank you very much. That is very kind of you. She works very hard at it. Margaret studies at home and I'm her teacher. I thought it would be interesting to show her our country's most important buildings."

"I'm a teacher as well," I said. "And I agree, nothing beats experiencing these places in person. Homeschooling is really admirable. I've met a lot of homeschool families and I really appreciate the sacrifices you make to educate your children directly."

"Thank you very much. It can be challenging at times, but so worth it. I am on call as a cardiologist at our hospital. On the days that I can't teach, Maddie meets with other families in our small town that also homeschool," Maddie's mom replied.

"Wow, a cardiologist and full-time teacher. I am really impressed. Hats off to you!" I said.

We stood together for a few minutes exchanging stories. When Tommy, Cam, and Freedom's grandfather came over, I asked Maddie and her mother if they would like to join us as we walked around the court. They agreed, and Freedom and her new BFF were immediately inseparable.

"Thank you for including us, Mr. Revere," Maddie said.

"Of course. We are thrilled to meet new friends," I replied.

Freedom nodded enthusiastically. "We could be pen pals, too. I'll send you my drawings. I do a really good one of my friend, Liberty. He's an amazing horse."

Maddie flashed a huge smile. "You have a horse? Wow, that is so cool."

Soon we passed through large oak doors into the Court Chamber. The view was stunning. Everything looked red and brown, and in the front of the room were nine chairs behind a raised wooden bench. American flags stood on either side. The Supreme Court was not in session, but when it was, this room would be packed.

"Some of the most important legal cases in our country's history were argued right here. Did you ever hear of the case *Brown v. Board of Education?*" Maddie's mom asked Maddie.

"I don't think so," Maddie said, and Freedom shrugged, too.

Maddie's mom continued: "It is the case that ended segregation based on race in the school system. The justices of the

Supreme Court said that it was against the Constitution to keep schoolchildren of different races separate, so thankfully the law was stopped."

Cam said, "So, when the Supreme Court justices lay down the law, they really lay down the law."

"Yes," Maddie's mom replied. "It is a very powerful court and they are powerful judges. They are part of the judicial branch of government. The legislative branch, or Congress, creates the laws, and the executive branch, or the President, enforces the laws. That is how the three branches work together and our freedoms are protected."

"Hey, when we met James Madison, he said the same thing about the three branches idea. And it came true!" Tommy said.

"Absolutely correct," I replied.

Maddie's mom looked at me, just like Benjameer did, as if Tommy was kidding about meeting Madison.

Tommy was busy secretly typing on his phone. When Freedom and Cam saw him they pulled out their own phones and started typing. The three beeps came again at almost the same time. I looked down at my phone and read *NINE JUSTICES, JUDICIAL BRANCH*. All were correct, but the first text came from Tommy, so he received the point.

When they finished, Freedom's grandfather said, "And don't forget about the Bill of Rights. The Supreme Court ensures that the rights such as freedom of speech, freedom of the press, and the freedom of religion are protected. Have you ever seen the police shows on TV?"

Cam responded, "Of course. I love those shows."

Freedom's grandfather said, "Well, in those shows, and in real life, when someone is arrested by the police they are read their rights. These rights are assured to every American citizen as part of the justices' decisions on the Bills of Rights. You probably know some of the words by heart. *You have the right to remain silent . . . you have the right to consult an attorney . . .*"

"Oh that's pretty cool," said Cam. "I didn't know where that came from but yeah, it's in every arrest scene."

We began walking toward the exit and soon we were out in the sun. It was a quick stroll to the park, where we found Liberty. As we approached, he made a drumroll with his hooves.

This caught the attention of Maddie and her mom. Their eyes went wide when Liberty said, "Congratulations, you have all successfully completed the Supreme Court objective of the mission. That means I have a prize for all of you. Want to know what it is?"

"Yes!" the Crew said in unison.

Maddie's mom's mouth was wide open in shock. I broke the silence by saying, "Um, Liberty, this is Maddie and her mom." I was looking at him sternly. He was clearly so excited he forgot to keep secret his ability to talk.

Maddie exclaimed, "I thought Freedom was just teasing me but . . . your horse really can talk!"

Maddie's mom had recovered a bit but still seemed flabbergasted. "Well, Mr. Revere, now I have seen everything," she said.

I nodded. "Yes, Liberty is, well, special. It's a long story, and I will fill you in on one condition."

"What condition, Mr. Revere?" Maddie asked.

"That you promise to stay in touch with us long distance as our pen pal and crew member," I replied.

Maddie's mom nodded approval.

"Yes, yes, I want to be part of the Crew!" Maddie exclaimed, her smile even brighter than before. "We could write letters and maybe send drawings and stuff. And I will be sure to keep it top secret."

"Awww," Liberty said, getting emotional. "But wait, don't you want to hear about the surprise?"

The kids all nodded their heads with energy.

Liberty raised his voice and said, "We are all going to see a Major League Baseball game!"

Everybody cheered, and after the noise settled, Maddie's mother came up beside me and said, "Thank you so much for including Maddie in the crew. She loves being a part of a team so much and meeting new friends. It can be challenging sometimes out of the traditional classroom setting."

"Of course, she will make a wonderful crew member," I said. "Speaking of team, we have some extra tickets to the baseball game today. If you and Maddie have time, we would love for you to join us."

Both Freedom and Maddie overheard my offer and said, "Please, please, pretty please?"

Maddie's mother agreed and Maddie and Freedom cheered.

Liberty piped in: "Don't forget we also had a winner from the Supreme Court mission objective. And the name of the secret agent who sent the correct text first: Tommy! That means Tommy is currently ahead by one point."

Tommy took a bow.

Liberty continued: "But there is still plenty of time left. I will see you guys at the ballpark!"

As we headed to the Metro station, Freedom gave her grandfather a hug and said, "I love having new friends."

I pulled the Crew aside to a quiet spot.

"Guys, I want to talk to you about something that will be difficult for you to understand. However, it is important," I said. "It is the issue of slavery in our country, which has been called America's original sin. Slavery was one of the most troubling issues at the Constitutional Convention in 1787.

"There is no excuse for it," I said sadly. "But learning history we must discuss it. So let me tell you this: the Founders added a section in the Constitution that outlawed the slave trade. However, it was done after a period of years rather than right away."

"But what about *all men are created equal?*" Tommy asked.

"There is no way to reconcile it, Cam. At the same time the Founders were fighting for freedom, slavery was allowed to continue. However, Benjamin Franklin and others were strongly opposed to slavery and created antislavery societies. It took a horrible Civil War to finally end it. When we get back to Manchester Middle School, we can talk about it more, okay?"

Everyone nodded.

After we spoke we took the Metro to Navy Yard station and walked the short distance to the ballpark. On the way we passed families in Washington Nationals gear, vendors, and food carts. The sun was shining and there was a cool breeze. It seemed like the perfect temperature. On the stadium a huge sign read NATIONALS.

"I am so pumped," said Cam. "I love baseball."

"Me, too! You think they'd let us play? Maybe run the bases?" Tommy asked.

"In your dreams," Cam said, slapping him on the back.

"Where's Liberty?" Maddie asked the group.

"That's a good question, Maddie," I replied. Hmmm, I thought, he was supposed to meet us the ballpark, but there was no sign of him yet.

"He's here already," said Freedom. "He told me he's going to take a nap by the side entrance so he doesn't get in the way."

That doesn't sound like Liberty, I thought, but hoped for the best.

As we entered the ballpark, I could smell the familiar aroma of hot dogs and peanuts. Cam asked to look at the seat numbers and led us through the walkway to our section.

As we walked through the entry into the field area, bright sunlight hit me in the face.

"Hey, these are great seats," Tommy said. "Pretty close to right behind home plate."

The crowd was huge—tens of thousands of people in a sea of red and white. People were turning to look at us as we passed. I knew my outfit stood out a bit, but I assumed people would think I was a team mascot or something—like from the New England Patriots.

Someone yelled, "Hey, Paul Revere, where's your horse?" and I felt my cheeks flush.

"They don't let horses inside the stadium!" Cam yelled back, and the crowd erupted in applause.

Another fan yelled, "Well done kid, you tell 'em!"

As we walked down the row to our seats I looked out onto the field. It was expertly raked and players were warming up or signing autographs. An American flag blew in the breeze near the scoreboard.

Suddenly, a voice came over the loudspeaker. It was a stadium announcer naming the players. We were close enough to read the backs of their jerseys as they lined up along the base lines.

"This is really cool, Mr. Revere," Cam said as his eyes darted from the crowd to the field and out to the scoreboard.

On the field players of both teams uniformly took off their hats and put them over their hearts.

"This is my favorite part," I whispered to Tommy.

"Me, too," he replied.

The stadium went from chattering to a hush. All were waiting for a woman with a microphone near the pitcher's mound to begin.

"See those men in military uniforms down by the singer?" I whispered to the group.

"Sure do," Freedom's grandfather replied.

"They are called the color guard. The guard formally escorts the American flag to and from the field. From the beginning, our military has presented the flag in this manner," I said.

"Yes, this is one of my favorite American traditions," Freedom's grandfather said, watching intently.

Cam added, "My dad is in the military and loves the color guard. I think he wanted to carry the flag but I'm not sure if he got the chance yet."

Taken by the mention of Cam's father, who I knew was deployed to Afghanistan, I said, "You should ask him. It is a huge honor. I am sure he would love to know you are interested in the color guard."

It was time for the National Anthem and Tommy took off his cap. Freedom's grandfather stood up straight. The whole stadium rose and focused on the American flag blowing gently in the distance.

Suddenly, the music began and a strong voice with a familiar melody came echoing through the stands.

> *O say can you see,*
> *By the dawn's early light,*
> *What so proudly we hailed*
> *At the twilight's last gleaming,*
> *Whose broad stripes and bright stars,*
> *Through the perilous fight,*
> *O'er the ramparts we watched,*
> *Were so gallantly streaming?*
> *And the rockets' red glare,*
> *The bombs bursting in air,*
> *Gave proof through the night*
> *That our flag was still there. . . .*

As the words blew through the air I watched the American flag waving red, white, and blue. People were singing along, including Tommy.

> *O say does that Star-Spangled Banner yet wave*
> *O'er the land of the free*
> *And the home of the brave?*

People of all backgrounds stood together, united and free. As the National Anthem ended, a thunderous roar of four military fighter jets rocketed over the ballpark. We all looked up to see the flyover and white vapor trail left in their wake. The crowd cheered wildly and the umpire yelled, "Play ball!"

"That was awesome!" yelled Tommy.

Freedom added, "Thank you for taking us to the game, Mr. Revere."

"I second that," said Freedom's grandfather. "You know, those jets remind me that many of our greatest athletes became soldiers during wartime."

"No way," said Tommy. "Is that true?"

"Absolutely," Freedom's grandfather answered. "Ted Williams was a Marine pilot in World War II during probably the best years of his career. He's a Hall of Famer. There are other athletes who made the same sacrifice."

"My grandpa said he would like to time-travel to meet Hall of Fame players when they were still playing. Wouldn't that be cool?" Tommy said.

Freedom's grandfather smiled, nodded, and patted Tommy on the shoulder.

The game remained tied into the fourth inning. Both teams had one run, and the pitching was tough, particularly the Nationals' young rookie pitcher, who had given up only two hits. As he wound up and released, it was clear he had a blazing fastball. Crack! The bat connected with the ball and it popped up into the air behind home plate. As we followed it, I had to shield my eyes from the sun.

"It's coming straight for us—look out, Maddie!" Freedom shouted, ducking her head.

I was too blinded to see anything.

"I wish I had a glove!" yelled Cam.

The next thing I knew, Tommy was reaching over my head with his hand. Thud! Tommy looked absolutely stunned as the foul ball landed perfectly in his baseball cap.

"Nooooooooo wayyyyyy!" Cam yelled.

The crowd around us cheered as Tommy lifted the ball out of his hat. He was smiling broadly, and the Fan Camera on a giant jumbotron screen showed him raising his hand and showing off his ball. The entire stadium could see the instant replay of the impressive catch.

"This one is for Grandpa. I know he would want to be here if he could," Tommy said.

I was immensely proud of Tommy. He was carrying a heavy heart but it did not stop him. He reminded me of the young Patriot we met after the Battle of Bunker Hill, still showing pride in his country despite the loss.

Maddie and Freedom were having a great time, laughing, whispering, and showing each other their sketches. It was as if they had known each other all their lives.

During the seventh inning stretch, I asked everyone if they would like something from the concessions. Unsurprisingly, everyone had an order.

"Mr. Revere, you'd have to be an octopus to carry all those drinks by yourself. I'll come with you and help," Tommy said, following behind.

"Be back soon," added Tommy. "Unless I get mobbed by all my adoring fans."

We found the nearest hot dog stand not too far from our seats. As we waited in line, I asked Tommy if he knew the meaning of the National Anthem. He sang all of the words so well, I assumed he knew what they meant.

"My grandfather taught me the anthem. He told me it's really important to take off your hat out of respect. I hear it a lot at my games, so I think I kinda know what it means," Tommy replied.

I smiled and said, "It's funny because a lot of people know the words and sing along but don't really know the meaning."

"How about we go on a special time-travel adventure?" I asked. "I have something incredible in mind that I think your grandfather would really like you to hear about."

Tommy's face lit up. "You mean just us?"

I nodded, "Yes, well, you, me, and Liberty, of course. We can tell the others about it when we get back."

"Okay, I'm in," Tommy said.

Before I could go into detail, a familiar voice behind us called out and said, "Hi, Thomas, even the back of your head looks cute!"

Oh no, I thought to myself. There's only one person I know who calls Tommy, *Thomas*. I groaned. "It can't be."

I turned around and could not believe my eyes. Tommy stood there like a frozen statue.

"I knew that was you on the jumbotron, Thomas," Elizabeth smirked. She wore her cheerleading sweats and her blond hair was pulled back in a bow.

"Wha-wha-what are you doing here?" asked Tommy in a stupor.

"Looking for you, silly," said Elizabeth. "I had no idea you were at the game until I saw your cute face on the big screen." She squeezed the left side of his face. "I was like, Oh. My. Gosh. That's my Thomas who caught that ball. I was so excited I just had to come and find you."

Tommy pulled off his cap and brushed his fingers through his hair. He was in thinking mode. He asked, "Yeah, but what are you doing in Washington, D.C.?"

Elizabeth moved closer and replied, "I had to come to this cheerleading competition in D.C. We totally took first place. It was so easy. And then our coach thought it was a good idea to come to a Nationals ball game. Boring. That is, until I saw you."

Tommy stood awkwardly, appearing to still be in shock.

Elizabeth looked me up and down and sneered, "Hello, Mr. Revere. I see you haven't found a new Halloween outfit."

"Wonderful to see you, too, Elizabeth," I said. I tried to be as polite as possible but I had reason to be cautious with Elizabeth.

Suddenly Maddie appeared at my side and said, "I'm sorry, Mr. Revere. I changed my mind. I don't want any popcorn." Freedom and Cam were standing beside her, and their expressions immediately turned to frowns.

Elizabeth looked straight at Freedom with a sarcastic glare and then, measuring up the rest of the Crew, she said, "If it isn't the Manchester Middle School Misfits." Elizabeth eyed Freedom's sketchpad and smiled. She talked as if speaking to a three-year-old and said, "Ah, isn't that cute. *Free-dumb* is learning to draw. Did you bring your crayons? Remember not to eat them. Maybe one day you could learn to be an artist."

"I *am* an artist," Freedom said, as Elizabeth looked her up and down.

I knew I needed to take control of the situation. "This is Elizabeth, a student from Manchester Middle School," I said.

"Oh, I know who she is," Cam muttered under his breath. "And I'd rather dive into a pool of fire ants than stick around here." Cam waved as he walked back to the seats.

"Oh, wow," Elizabeth said, rolling her eyes. "I knew the Little Rascals couldn't be far if Thomas is here."

"This is Maddie, our new friend," I said. "Maddie, Elizabeth is a student at Manchester Middle School and is in Washington, D.C., for a cheerleading competition."

"We won, of course. Something that *losers* can't quite appreciate," Elizabeth said, as she glanced at everyone but Tommy.

Elizabeth leaned in and whispered to Maddie, "Your new friends put the uncool in school. I can see that they rubbed off on you."

Freedom stared at Elizabeth and said, "That's enough, Elizabeth. Maddie has more cool in her little finger than you do in your whole body. Why don't you go back to your cheer squad and leave us alone?"

"Okay, simmer down," Elizabeth said. "I'll go, but only if my handsome knight Thomas escorts me."

Tommy turned bright red.

"Good luck, Sir Thomas," Freedom said, smiling, as she and Maddie left to go back to their seats.

Tommy turned to Elizabeth and said, "Uh, how about we try to meet up after the game, before we head back to our hotel?"

Elizabeth sighed but smiled. "Fine, but don't miss me too much," she said, batting her eyelashes.

As Elizabeth walked away I said, "You're really not planning to meet her after the game, are you?"

"Not if I can help it," Tommy replied. "But I would love to go on that field trip now."

"I think I can arrange that," I said, smiling.

As we left the ballpark, we saw to our total amazement that Liberty was actually where he said he would be.

"Liberty, fancy seeing you here in the proper spot. For that, you get two apples and a carrot," I said.

"Wowza, I should try listening more often," Liberty replied. He crunched on the apples like a puppy receiving a treat. "So, what's the plan, Captain?"

"We're headed to 1814, Baltimore Harbor, near Fort McHenry," I said. "We are searching for Francis Scott Key."

I gave Tommy his colonial clothes to put over his modern ones.

"You got it, Captain," said Liberty as we walked toward a secluded spot. He then took a deep breath and shouted, *"Rush, rush, rushing to history!"*

Chapter 9

The time portal opened and Liberty jolted forward so abruptly I didn't have time to put my feet in the stirrups. I was looking down and not paying attention when he jumped. In the next second he landed on a wooden floor and instantly jerked to a sudden stop.

My momentum carried me up and over Liberty, through a dark and musty room, until I did a somersault midair and crashed feetfirst through the top of a large wooden barrel. My shoes smashed through the lid.

"Nice move, Mr. Revere," said Tommy, still sitting in Liberty's saddle. "You've got to teach me that flying ninja trick. I didn't know you could do that."

Neither did I, I thought.

Tommy scrunched up his nose about the same time I did. "Something smells like pickles," he said.

"Oh, I love pickles," said Liberty. "Dill pickles, sweet pickles, bread and butter pickles, even spicy pickle relish. Yum."

The dim light from a lantern that hung from some nearby stairs gave off just enough light for us to see that I was indeed standing in a barrel of pickles with pickle juice up to my shins.

Liberty tried to cheer things up and said, "The good news is that pickles are low in cholesterol and a very good source of dietary fiber."

"When we get back to modern day we should give your pickled socks to Elizabeth," Tommy said, chuckling. "She deserves them."

All of a sudden the entire room lit up and we heard a loud, deep bang. It sounded like fireworks on the Fourth of July. Liberty's eyes got wide and Tommy turned his head quickly toward the door. The light from outside flashed and then went dark, like someone turning on and off a light switch. But there were no light switches in 1814; Thomas Edison had not been born yet.

"Ahhhhhh!" shrieked Liberty. "Is the floor tilting below us? Is this an earthquake?" The ground shifted to one side and then the other. Barrels and crates were stacked on either side of us. When a roll of cheese skipped past, Liberty shrieked again.

"Those sounds must be bombs exploding in the harbor," I said.

"Bombs? That's not very safe," Tommy said.

"We are on a British ship in the middle of Baltimore Harbor in the middle of the War of 1812," I said.

"Wait, did you say a British ship?! Why a British ship? 1812? Did Liberty mess up?" Tommy asked.

"I heard that," Liberty said. "Wait, wait, wait just a minute. I may be surrounded by pickle juice but I landed exactly where I was supposed to."

I carefully lifted one foot out of the pickle barrel and onto the wobbly ground until both shoes were pickle-free.

"Easy cheesy," I said, channeling my inner Liberty. "Yes, we landed in the correct location. The War of 1812 was still being fought in 1814. A little confusing, I know, but I believe Francis Scott Key is somewhere on this boat. As history tells us, he came aboard to help an American doctor named Beanes, who was arrested by the British."

"So this may be a really dumb question, but why is he still here?" Tommy asked. "I mean, why didn't he help and then leave ASAP?"

I smiled and said, "You would think he would, wouldn't you? Unfortunately, while he worked to release Dr. Beanes, the Battle of Fort McHenry began and he was stuck."

In the next flash of light I crouched toward a slat in the door and looked out. I could see the faint outlines of the deck of a ship.

"What's going on outside?" asked Tommy.

I waved him over to look through the slats in the door, and saw the outlines of two Redcoats walking up and down the deck with guns on their shoulders. British boats filled the harbor like ducks at a family gathering.

"Whoa, I don't know what's more scary, the bombs or the Redcoats pacing out there," Tommy said nervously. "I can't believe we are back in a battle!"

"See all those huge boats in the harbor?" I said. "They are some of the largest ships in the British Royal Navy and they are firing thousands of bombs on the American fort named McHenry. Right now in history, the United States is at war again with Great Britain, twenty-seven years after we visited James Madison in Philadelphia in 1787."

"This is like the longest football game ever. Except it's not a game," Tommy said. "They must be really tired of fighting."

"Yes, I am sure they are. But the Americans are very determined to hold on to the freedoms they gained during the American Revolution," I said.

Tommy crouched, looked out, and said, "Remember when we met William Bradford on the *Mayflower*?"

I was thrilled that our first adventure to Plymouth Plantation in 1620 made such a lasting impression on Tommy. "That's right," I said. "The Pilgrims made the voyage across the rough seas in search of freedom. Here, almost two hundred years later, the American people are still fighting to preserve them."

A loud crunching noise could be heard behind us.

"Mmm, these pickles are scrumptious," said Liberty, munching over the opened barrel. "I mean a little too salty but still really good."

Boom! Boom! Boom! The bangs seemed louder this time.

"How can you eat at a time like this?" Tommy asked.

"C'mon, Tommy, we need to sneak out onto the deck and find Francis Scott Key," I said. "If we wait until the British patrol passes, we can sneak outside. Liberty, you'd better stay here. It's too hard to hide a horse on a ship."

Tommy quietly opened the door and looked out. He whispered, "Grandpa will definitely not believe me when he sees these notes."

"I think I've had enough," said Liberty, who looked a lot rounder in the belly. "Seriously, I think I ate too many pickles. They were so good but I just remembered pickles make me gassy. But don't worry. I'll give you fair warning before . . . well, you know. Before I have to, um, degasify."

I rolled my eyes.

"Uh-oh," said Liberty. "I really shouldn't have eaten so many pickles. Seriously, you should have stopped me. Friends don't let friends eat that many pickles."

Tommy started to laugh and said, "Hey, Liberty, I have a tongue twister for you."

"Okay, but you better make it fast. These pickles are starting to talk to me, if you know what I'm saying," Liberty exclaimed.

"Okay, here it is," said Tommy. "Peter Piper picked a peck of pickled peppers; a peck of pickled peppers Peter Piper picked. If Peter Piper picked a peck of pickled peppers, where's the peck of pickled peppers Peter Piper picked?"

Liberty raised an eyebrow. "That's a good one. But the word *pickled* has only accelerated the fumigation countdown. Twenty, nineteen, eighteen, seventeen . . ."

"Let's go, Tommy," I whispered, hurriedly. "Quietly open the door and tell me what you see."

Liberty continued his countdown, "Eleven, ten, nine, eight . . ."

"Is the coast clear?" I said, nervously. I had been around Liberty when he was gassy before, and let's just say it's not something I wanted to experience again.

Another bang in the sky lit up the ship giving us a clear view. I said, "Deck's clear; let's go now!"

"Five, four, three . . ." Liberty counted.

Tommy and I ran toward the mast of the ship. Just as we got to the other side, footsteps of British soldiers pounded across the deck toward the door we just exited. We crouched behind some wooden crates and observed the closed door to the pickle room. I hoped Liberty would turn invisible in time!

Suddenly the door creaked. "What's that noise?" said one of the soldiers.

"It's coming from inside the storage room," said the other.

The soldier in front began to open the door, and as he did I turned to Tommy and whispered, "Here it comes."

Tommy grinned, "I hope nobody lights a match."

The soldier cried out, "Ugh! Knock me into a cocked hat; what's that smell?"

The second soldier gagged. "Good heavens! It smells like a sewer of rotten pickles. You should go in and check it out."

"I'm not taking my smeller down there," said the first.

Tommy covered his mouth and tried not to laugh out loud.

"Liberty's making the perfect diversion," I said.

Again, the sky lit up like fireworks on the Fourth of July.

"Wow, look at that," Tommy exclaimed as something streaked across the sky and exploded, falling into bits and pieces of light toward the ground. "Are you sure this is safe, Mr. Revere? I mean, the fireworks make me think it's a holiday and we should be barbecuing but those are real bombs, right?"

In the distance we could make out a small building on the end of a stretch of land, shaped like a star.

"Yes, it's beautiful, if it were not so dangerous," I replied. "But we're safe here. The fort you see in the distance is Fort McHenry. There, a small group of Americans led by General Armistead is determined to defend the city of Baltimore from the British."

"Mr. Revere, why are we looking for Francis Scott Key right now? Shouldn't we wait until the battle ends and find him somewhere else?"

"Normally I would agree, but tonight, September 13, 1814, Francis Scott Key writes our national anthem. We need to find out exactly what inspired him to write it."

"Oh, wow," Tommy replied, "I'm in."

We crawled from behind the boxes and made our way closer to the railing. There, we found a ladder and snuck down to a quieter section of the deck away from the growing number of soldiers. Cannons continued to fire around us, and as one lit up the sky, we saw a man thoughtfully pacing back and forth. He was tall and around his mid-thirties, well dressed, and definitely not a British soldier. He stopped to look out over the ship's railing toward Fort McHenry. Then, he brought a retractable handheld telescope up to his eye and slowly scanned the bombardment of Baltimore.

"Look, I think that's Francis Scott Key," I said.

"I should ask him to sign my baseball," Tommy joked, pulling the ball he caught at the Nationals game from his pocket.

I laughed, "How did you sneak that . . ."

Suddenly, the ship tilted to one side. We both stumbled and Tommy lost his grip on the ball. It dropped to the deck and rolled directly toward Key. The ball hit his right boot, causing him to look down. Curiously, he picked it up and tried to study it in the darkness.

Tommy didn't waste any time. He jumped to his feet and ran toward the ball. "Sorry about that, Mr. Key. I accidentally dropped my baseball."

Francis Scott Key forced a smile and handed the ball to Tommy. "I'm not familiar with a *baseball*," He said, "I'm sorry, have we met before?"

"Oh, um, well no," Tommy said, looking at me nervously.

I said, "We apologize for interrupting you. I am Rush Revere, a history teacher. This is my student, Tommy."

Lights continued to flash in the sky, and cannons boomed. A light rain started to fall.

Along with writing the national anthem, this exceptional American
was also a leading attorney in Washington, and he fought as a soldier
in the War of 1812. It is Francis Scott Key.

"My name is Francis Scott Key. It is a pleasure to meet you. There are few of us Americans on this prison ship, but I am hopeful we will be returned to Baltimore soon. Much depends on Fort McHenry. By tomorrow we will know our fate." He paused and sniffed the air. "That's odd. I think I smell pickles." Thankfully, he didn't give it too much thought.

Key turned away toward Baltimore and nervously looked through his spyglass. "Yes, good, it is a relief to see the American flag still flying. Here, young man. Take a look through this spyglass."

Tommy put the glass up to his eye. After a few seconds he said, "I can see it. There is a big storm, and the flag is really waving hard."

"Do you know what it means, young man, if that American flag is *not* flying?" asked Key.

"I'm not really sure. Do they take it down in the rain?" Tommy asked.

Key smiled, "No, that is a small storm flag, and it is raised during battles or bad weather. It will come down only if the Americans lose control of Fort McHenry."

"Are the Americans fighting back?" Tommy asked.

"They are trying, but their guns do not have the range to reach the British in the harbor. The Royal Navy ships have fired thousands of bombs and rockets at the Americans for almost a full day. They plan to destroy Fort McHenry and force a surrender." I felt my heart beating fast as Francis Scott Key spoke.

"So if the Americans lose the fort, they will lose the whole war?" Tommy asked.

"That is right," Key said. "And we will be forced to again swear allegiance to the King, the same one who burned our Capitol to the ground."

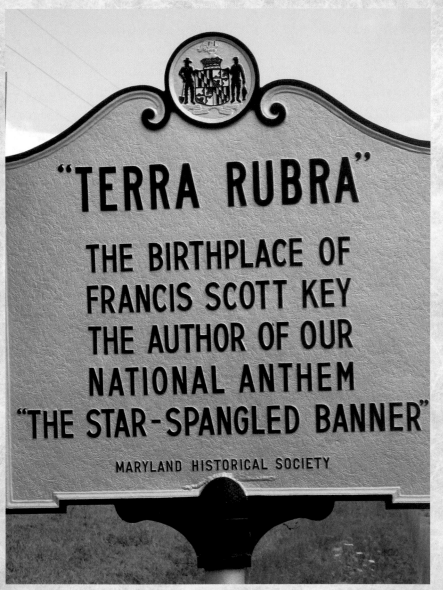

Terra Rubra is the birthplace of Francis Scott Key.
He was born August 1, 1779, in Carroll County, Maryland.

As the rain continued to fall I was glad we were wearing coats.

The bombing grew heavier. Nearly every second, a cannon was shot or a rocket was fired. I wondered how long Fort McHenry could hold out. The British Navy was the strongest in the world, and these were like modern-day battleships.

Francis Scott Key must have been thinking the same thing because he turned around and took a deep breath. His hand was shaking as he pulled out a letter and a pen. On the back of a piece of paper he began scribbling. It was too dark to see what was on the page.

I said, "Mr. Key, could I ask what you are writing?"

He paused for a moment and replied, "I sometimes write poetry." His smile was calm, but his shoulders were wet and slumped. A cool night breeze pushed across the deck. "My children seem to enjoy the little rhymes. I would rather be in Fort McHenry fighting, but I am stuck here. So I will write a few lines to remember this night, in case our freedom is lost forever."

We stood quietly and watched the sky light up again. In a trembling hand, Francis Scott Key held a piece of paper as raindrops fell onto a small roof above us. In the light, I could now read the words,

Can you see by the light of dawn, the pride in twilight's gleam?

Tommy looked at me confused, and said, "Mr. Key, I thought you were going to write about the battle. Why did you write about the dawn and the light?"

Mr. Key smiled through tired eyes. "You remind me of my children, Tommy. They are always asking wonderful questions like yours. At twilight, or when the sun goes down until dawn, is the worst part of the battle for the Americans. If they hold out throughout the night, they still have a chance. I am asking, in this poem, if the American flag that flew at twilight will still be there in the morning."

At that, Francis Scott Key appeared to hit on an idea and wrote—

Oh say can you see by the dawn's early light
What so proudly we hailed at the twilight's last gleaming?

I was mesmerized. Francis Scott Key had just written the words of our national anthem, and goose bumps covered my arms.

Tommy pointed to a section on the page of Francis Scott Key's notes and asked, "What is a *perilous* fight?"

"Perilous means extremely dangerous, and that is exactly what General Armistead is facing inside Fort McHenry. We do not know how many soldiers have been lost, and right now, the British Army is approaching by land. Everything now depends on a tiny group fighting a perilous fight. The question is, how long can they hold on?"

Tommy said, "I understand. It is like a football game, where you're tired. You're ahead by a point, but the other team keeps marching down the field. You're just holding on until the final whistle."

Before Key could respond, the light flashed again. I glimpsed the next section of the page that read,

The bombs bursting in air,
Gave proof through the night
That our flag was still there.

Tommy pointed to the words. "What does it mean about the bombs giving proof?"

Mr. Key responded, "It means that when the British guns fall silent we will know if the troops at Fort McHenry survived the night. If everything goes quiet, one of two things has happened—either the British have won, and our cause is lost, or our flag is still flying, and we have kept our freedom."

"But how will we know which one it is?" Tommy asked, earnestly.

"We will wait until the British guns stop firing. At that moment, we will look through the spyglass. If the American flag is still waving over Fort McHenry we have won the battle."

At that, Key quickly scribbled on his paper the immortal words—

Oh, say does that star-spangled banner yet wave,
O'er the land of the free and the home of the brave?

I asked to borrow Francis Scott Key's spyglass and looked through the circular view toward Fort McHenry. As I did I took a deep breath. The waves pushed my view up and down so I steadied myself against the railing. Through the glass, I first saw the ramparts, or walls of Fort McHenry, and then, in the center, a small American flag.

Key said, "Our flag is still there, for now. Let us meet here immediately after the guns fall silent. We will hope for the best. Right now, I need to speak with Dr. Beanes. Try to get some sleep my friends. Good evening." He turned and vanished into the darkness.

"Wow," said Tommy. "I hope the morning gets here soon, because I am way too excited to sleep."

"I'm way too excited to sleep, too," announced Liberty as he appeared right next to us.

"Hi, Liberty," said Tommy, cheerfully. "You just missed Francis Scott Key, the author of our national anthem. He was awesome!"

"All is well in the storage room, I presume?" I asked.

Liberty gave a half-smile and said, "That is highly gasified information. But, yes, I'm feeling much better. Oh, and I had to come up with a reason why it smelled so bad below deck, so I smashed a barrel of pickles. I made it look like the barrel just exploded on its own. Anyway, there's like ten British soldiers cleaning up the mess. I doubt we'll be bothered for a while."

The ship continued to move up and down, and the dark outlines of the British Navy remained in the harbor. We found a spot in a hidden section of the ship with some leftover straw that looked like an old barn. Tommy and I each found a corner. At some point I fell asleep among the exploding lights above Baltimore while Liberty kept watch through the rest of the night.

Before I knew it someone nudged my shoulder. I was still too tired to open my eyes until a long wet tongue that smelled like pickles licked my face.

"Liberty," I said, firmly, "I'm awake. What's happening?"

"That's just it," Liberty said. "Nothing's happening. Listen."

My eyes went wide and I quickly turned to shake Tommy. "Tommy, wake up. The bombing has stopped."

Tommy jerked awake and we both stood and ran out the door to the ship's railing where we last saw Francis Scott Key. We stared across the water at Fort McHenry. The sun had just started to peek over the horizon.

Liberty disappeared and two seconds later Francis Scott Key

walked over to us and said, "Good morning." He looked ragged and his eyes were red. His coat was still wet.

"Good morning," we replied. No other words were needed. The guns were silent, and we all knew what this meant. Mr. Key looked concerned. He took a long deep breath and said, "I have horrible news to report. A moment ago, I looked over the ramparts of the fort, and the American flag was not flying. On the flagpole, there is now an empty space."

My shoulders sank. Had we somehow changed history?

"We lost?" Tommy asked in disbelief. "I thought we won. I mean, I thought we were going to win," he corrected.

"I am afraid so," said Key. "Shortly, the British flag is sure to be raised."

My heart was racing, but without the spyglass, I could only make out blurry outlines of the fort. In the stillness, we could hear the faint sound of waves lapping against the side of the ship.

Tommy said, "Maybe there is hope, Mr. Key. There is always hope, right?"

Mr. Key looked at Tommy and said quietly, "Yes, there is always hope, Tommy."

At that, Francis Scott Key raised the spyglass slowly to his eye. After what seemed like hours, his shoulders sank, he lowered his head, and placed his hands firmly on the railing. He was shaking as he handed me the spyglass. British ships swayed menacingly all around us.

I took a deep breath, put the spyglass to my eye, and found the fort's flagpole in the distance.

"What is it, Mr. Revere?" Tommy asked, "Can you see the British flag?"

Through the circle of the spyglass I saw it; a flag lying limply halfway up the tall pole above Fort McHenry. The sky was becoming light behind it. It was the red and blue of the British flag. What had we done?

As the flag was being raised, a gust of wind blew. I took a long deep breath as the flag fluttered in the wind. I put the spyglass down and turned to Tommy.

"What is it, Mr. Revere? What's wrong?"

"It's just . . . there are stars on the flag, Tommy," I said.

"What does that mean?" Tommy asked as I handed him the spyglass.

Francis Scott Key lifted his head and looked directly at me.

"The British flag does not have stars, Tommy," Key said. "The troops at Fort McHenry have defeated the mighty British Navy. The American flag is still flying!" Then a gust of wind blew, and the flag opened wide. It was enormous! Large enough to see without a spyglass.

Tommy yelled, "The British ships are turning away!"

For the next hour, we watched the mighty British Navy sail out of Baltimore Harbor.

As the sun rose high over the water, the star-spangled banner still waved over the land of the free and the home of the brave.

BETSEY ROSS

Betsy Ross is seen here sewing the American flag.
Mary Pickersgill, another flag maker, created the Star-Spangled Banner
that flew over Fort McHenry in 1814.

Chapter 10

My heart felt like it was dancing as we time-jumped back to Nationals ballpark in modern day. We came back right after we first left.

Liberty quickly ran off for a bathroom break, assuring us he would stay right where we left him just outside the gate.

"I can't wait to tell my grandpa about Francis Scott Key and the National Anthem. Now whenever I hear the anthem playing before a game, I'll be thinking about the words—especially where they were written," Tommy said.

We made our way through the stadium and back to our seats, where the rest of the Crew were waiting.

Freedom sniffed the air and asked, "Does anyone else smell pickles?"

"Must be the pickle relish on my hot dog," said Cam.

"Yep, that's some strong pickle relish," Tommy said, winking at me. Freedom's grandpa raised an eyebrow as he glanced at my soiled boots.

"Where's Eliza-brat?" Cam asked.

"Please tell me she's not coming back anytime soon," Freedom said.

"We left her with her cheerleading team. She said she'd see us later but hopefully we can slip out of here first," Tommy said.

The final innings of the game were uneventful. When the game ended, the crowd began to leave.

"That was an awesome game, Mr. Revere," said Cam.

"Yeah, it's really cool that the Nationals won," Maddie agreed.

As we stood to leave our row, I tapped Tommy on the shoulder and pointed to the field. The American flag took on new meaning for me as it waved. We absorbed the scene, as Maddie and Freedom stood side by side chatting.

After gathering our belongings, we headed up the stairs. It was time to bid farewell to Maddie and her mother.

When we reached the exit, Freedom gave Maddie a big hug. "Don't forget to write," she said.

We waved goodbye to our new friends until they disappeared into the crowd.

"All right, crew. Let's go find Liberty," I said, patting Freedom on the shoulder. She looked a little down.

When we arrived at the prearranged meeting spot, Liberty was nowhere to be found. We scanned the area until my eye landed on something big, brown, and white wearing a Nationals baseball cap. He came trotting toward us, huffing and puffing. "Phew, that was close," Liberty said.

"What was?" I asked, reluctantly.

"I was napping just outside the stadium when I overhead someone say Tommy's name. I opened my eyes and saw Elizabeth and her group of cheerleaders prancing by," Liberty said.

"But don't worry, she didn't see me. I was in disguise with my baseball cap."

"Where did you get the cap?" I asked, accusingly.

"Hey, I didn't steal it, if that's what you're implying. A nice lady saw me standing out here and thought I would look cute with a hat on."

Freedom smiled and patted Liberty on the nose.

"So what is the next objective of the mission?" Freedom's grandfather asked.

Freedom pulled out her mission card. "It looks like we are going to the White House," she said. "My card says that Liberty will give us the clue when we get there."

I motioned for the Crew to gather around and pulled out a twenty-dollar bill to show everyone a picture of the White House.

"That's cool," said Cam. "I never noticed it was on the twenty. Speaking of numbers, where are we on the mission points, Commander Liberty?"

"You and Freedom are behind by one point," Liberty said.

"Can we go to the White House tonight?" Freedom asked.

"It is getting a little late," I replied. "How about we go get some dinner at the hotel and rest tonight? First thing in the morning we will visit the White House. Sound good?"

The Crew and Freedom's grandfather all nodded happily.

"Oh, and Liberty, this will give you some time to work on tomorrow's clue," I said.

"An actor as great as me needs very little practice, Revere," Liberty said.

"Of course," I said, and bowed melodramatically.

"We'll take the Metro and meet you at the hotel. I assume your Spidey-sense will help you find your way back," I joked.

Can you name the building on the back of this twenty-dollar bill?

Liberty rolled his eyes. "Does the earth need help rotating around the sun? I can't wait to check into my suite! Luxury bed and room service, here I come!"

"I hate to burst your bubble but I don't think the hotel will look too kindly on a horse walking through their lobby. I am sure there is a comfy spot for you to sleep in the garage," I replied. "I'll even order you a veggie entrée and bring it out to you."

Liberty pouted.

"How about we head to the Metro?" I said, changing the subject.

After a brief trip on the underground train, we made it back to our hotel. The Crew was walking more slowly than earlier in the day.

The next morning, we gathered for breakfast in the hotel café.

"You know what I most love about buffets?" Freedom asked. "The cinnamon rolls."

"Oh, where are those? I missed them," Cam said, heading back to the buffet. He returned with a plate piled high.

"Well, well, well," a voice said chillingly behind us, "are those all for you?"

"Oh no," Freedom whispered. "What is *she* doing here?"

Elizabeth was walking toward our table, with her nose in the air.

"I thought you were going to wait for me at the game, Thomas," Elizabeth said, with a sigh.

Tommy looked like a puppy dog who just got scolded for chewing on the garden hose.

"Good morning, Elizabeth, what a nice surprise," I said, trying to be diplomatic.

Elizabeth pulled up a chair and sat at our table. She said, "I thought it was very rude of you to not say goodbye after the game. It's a good thing Tommy told me what hotel you were staying at."

"That was a big mistake," Cam said under his breath.

"I heard that, Cameron," Elizabeth said. "My cheer coach brought me here so I could spend the morning with you. She'll be back to get me. But to be perfectly honest, I'm here for Thomas. I know he missed me." She reached for a pitcher of orange juice and filled Tommy's glass.

"Oh," said Tommy, sheepishly. "Thanks."

The table grew quiet until Freedom's grandfather broke the silence and said, "Since you are joining us, you should know we plan to visit the White House this morning."

"Perfect," said Elizabeth, hanging by Tommy's side.

After a few minutes we exited the hotel. I whispered to Freedom to tell Liberty to meet us at the north gate of the White House.

By the time we approached the White House everyone seemed exasperated with Elizabeth.

Cam asked, "Hey, Lizzy, what kind of perfume are you wearing? I bet it's strong enough to keep away lions and tigers and bears."

Freedom chuckled.

Elizabeth flipped her perfectly combed blond hair over her designer jacket and said, "You are so funny, Cameron. I wish I had your sense of humor because then I could scare away a stampede of elephants. Hey, speaking of elephants, where's your ridiculous horse?"

"He's meeting us at the White House," I said and then mumbled, "and I'm sure he'll be thrilled to see you."

From a distance I could make out the outline. There were buildings all around us as we walked, but the official residence and principal workplace of the President stood out in contrast to all around it. The majestic symbol of American freedom was surrounded by green, with tall trees flanking all sides.

We walked through Lafayette Square, past a statue of President Andrew Jackson, toward the front of the White House. As we approached the perimeter iron gates, we could see the wide lawn directly in front of the White House.

"Wow, there it is!" yelled Tommy, scaring a tourist who was taking a picture beside him.

The Crew peered through the open slots in the gates. I could not quite make out the beautiful rose garden or the president's helicopter landing pad, but I knew they were there.

"This is unbelievable. The President's house is right there," Tommy observed. "Oh, and look, Mr. Revere, there is the flag right on top in the center."

"Is the president in there right now?" Cam asked.

"You know I am not sure. But there are definitely lots and lots of people working inside. The president is surrounded by a cabinet or team that help him to carry out the daily tasks of his job as leader of the free world."

"So cool!" Freedom's grandfather said, absorbing the moment.

I added, "Do you know that every president takes an oath of office that is written in Article II of the Constitution? Have you heard this before: . . . *that I will faithfully execute the Office of the President of the United States, and will to the best of my Ability, preserve, protect and defend the Constitution of the United States?* It is a promise to the people of the country."

The president of the United States lives and works in this building, the White House. Do you know the shape of the president's office?

We stood admiring all the details of the grand building, along with crowds of tourists. I looked at the fountains, and the hedges, the flowers, the large windows, and the incredible columns right in front of the main house doors.

"Regardless of politics or who is the president at the time, I have such admiration for the position and what it means in our country. President of the United States is a huge title and responsibility," Freedom's grandfather said, looking on. I nodded in full agreement.

After a few minutes I heard the clomping of hooves on the asphalt.

"Hey, Revere, you all look very rested. I'm not jealous, nope, not at all," Liberty said, "I had a wonderful sleep smelling car fumes in the parking garage. Ummmm no." He squinted both eyes.

"Why, good morning, sunshine. If it isn't the most chipper horse I've ever seen. How about you deliver the next clue in the mission? That will cheer you up," I said, smiling through Liberty's stare.

"Yeahhh, I need some points!" Cam exclaimed.

"Me, too!" Freedom joined in.

Liberty's face changed instantly and his voice lowered. "Secret agents, the time is now. This is make or break. As this is your final clue, it is worth double points! The current tally is Cam with two points, Tommy with two points, and Freedom with one point. So anyone can win!" After a long pause he pointed a hoof toward the White House. "There is the President's House; it is important in the mission objective. The clue is:

The president lives in the White House. What is the street address?

The National Archives is located on Constitution Avenue. Fitting, isn't it?
It received its name on February 26, 1931.

"Let's go in and find out. I need to keep my winning streak!" Tommy bragged.

We began to walk up to the entrance. "Oh no, that sign says no tours to the public today," Freedom said.

Freedom's grandfather took a closer look and said, "There seems to be a private function going on today."

"That's such a bummer," said Tommy. "I really wanted to see the Egg Office."

"It's called the Oval Office," corrected Freedom.

"No, I don't think so," said Tommy. "It's the shape of an egg, right?"

Cam smiled, "Yeah, Freedom, it's called the Egg Office of the President."

"Oh wait, really?" asked Tommy, looking surprised and pleased with himself.

"Yeah, it's totally in the history books. But then Humpty Dumpty lost the presidency so they changed it."

Tommy slugged his friend in the arm. "Dude, c'mon. I can't believe I fell for that."

Cam laughed with Freedom and her grandfather.

"Oh, Thomas, you're so funny," said Elizabeth, giggling.

Freedom rolled her eyes and said, "So really, what exactly happens in the Oval Office?"

I smiled and replied, "It is the official office of the President and his primary place to work on major topics that are happening within our country. He is able to meet with his senior advisors and members of his cabinet right there."

"Here's some fun trivia about the Oval Office," Freedom's grandfather chimed in. "Did you know that each president decorates the Oval Office to his own personal tastes?"

Do you know what office is seen in the photo above?
It is a replica of the Oval Office, found at the Reagan Library.

"Mmm," said Liberty, dreamily. "Taste Oval Egg Office. Yummy."

"Um, I think Liberty is dreaming about the Oval Office. He's probably licking the walls," Tommy joked.

Freedom's grandfather continued: "And the Oval Office desk is made out of wood from a British navy ship that was presented to President Rutherford B. Hayes by the Queen way back in 1880. Since then, every president has used the same desk, with the exception of three. It is called the *Resolute* desk."

Freedom looked up at her grandpa with clear admiration.

"Which one is the Oval Office?" Freedom asked.

I pointed and replied, "The Oval Office is in the West Wing over there. The President and his family live in the residence between the West and East Wings. Even though we can't go in today, tours of the White House typically start on the East Wing."

Behind us a small group of people were waving signs attached to wooden sticks. They were shouting and clapping their hands, all wearing the same color shirts. At first I couldn't tell what they were doing.

Freedom's grandfather said, "I recognize this group from the news; they are protesting the law that bans smoking in federal buildings. They think American citizens should be able to smoke anywhere they want."

As the protestors got closer, I could read the backs of their T-shirts. *Smoke here, smoke there, smoke anytime, anywhere.* They were chanting the words, sounding like a broken record.

"Pee-yew, I hate smoking and I especially hate smoking inside," Elizabeth said, holding her nose. "How stupid are these people? They should be arrested and taken to jail for being so gross."

"Actually, they have the right to say whatever they want as Americans," Cam said. "Ever heard of George Mason and the Bill of Rights, Elizabeth? Freedom of speech is one of the big ones. They have a right in this country to speak their minds, even if kinda dumb."

"Very close Cam," I said. "The First Amendment to the U.S. Constitution stops the government from passing laws that prevent you from speaking your mind."

"Whatever," Elizabeth said, putting a hand on her hip. "This is exactly why I like King George. He would never put up with this stupidity. He would send them all to the Tower of London. I bet they would enjoy their smoking there."

"You certainly have a right to your opinion, Elizabeth. That, too, is guaranteed in the Bill of Rights. Now for a quick review," I said. "Congress passes a no-smoking law. Remember that is the legislative branch. The Supreme Court says the law is okay under the Constitution. That is the judicial branch. The president then makes sure the law is carried out and no one smokes in buildings. That is the executive branch."

"That is exactly what James Madison talked about," Tommy said.

"Right, but there is another group you need to know about. That is the people themselves—us. We can vote for new representatives in Congress, and we can protest in the streets. In that way we protect our own freedoms."

Elizabeth rolled her eyes. "I still think we should lock them up and throw away the key. And then we can burn those hideous-looking T-shirts."

"When do we eat the Oval Office?" Liberty said groggily.

"Liberty, wake up," I said, nudging harder.

Liberty jerked awake.

"Hey we forgot about the mission objective," Tommy said.

Cam added, "Yeah, how are we going to find the address? I don't see a number or sign or anything."

Freedom did not say anything but was walking toward the perimeter gate in front of the White House.

"I already looked there, Freedom. There no address!" Tommy yelled, but she did not turn around.

Once she got to the gate I saw her approach a policeman. Beside him was a police dog who looked up at her. We all quickly walked over toward them, with the exception of Liberty, who was momentarily distracted by an ice cream cart in the distance.

"Sir, could I ask you a question?" Freedom said politely to the police officer.

"Of course, young lady, go ahead," the officer replied.

"What address is this? I mean what address is the White House?" she asked.

The policeman smiled at us and said, "Oh good question. I will give you a hint. Divide 3,200 by two and add the name of the state where Philadelphia is located, then add 'Avenue' to the end of it. That is your answer."

"Thank you, sir," Freedom said, looking a little confused, and pulled out her sketchpad and pencil. She did some quick math, and caught up with Tommy, who was already heading back toward Liberty. Cam followed right behind.

Freedom's grandfather and I made our way back as quickly as we could, to see the Crew surrounding Liberty.

"Sixteen Hundred Pennsylvania Avenue!" Cam and Tommy shouted, before Freedom had a chance to say anything. She put her hands on her hips and shook her head.

Liberty looked at both boys and then at Freedom. I thought it was unfair that she found the answer and the boys outran her back to Liberty.

"Well, Cam and Tommy, you have succeeded in your mission," Liberty said with great drama. Cam and Tommy high-fived each other while Freedom looked at her grandfather. He gave her a look back as if to say, "It's okay."

Liberty continued. "And Cam and Tommy tied in being first to deliver their answer. So, that would mean that you and Tommy are tied for first place . . ." Tommy and Cam smiled. "But . . ." Liberty said taking a long pause. "But, the winner of the mission and our new Super Scout is . . . FREEDOM!"

The boys looked at her dumbfounded, as she smiled sweetly in their direction. Freedom's grandfather and I looked at each other, confused.

"Wait, what happened?" Cam asked, "She didn't say anything."

"No she didn't," said Liberty, "but she did *text* '1600 Pennsylvania Avenue, home of the president to be exact.' And I received it thirty seconds before you shouted it."

Freedom took a little bow as we all clapped.

"Girl power!" Freedom said. "I wish Maddie was here to celebrate with."

"Well done, Freedom," both boys said, as we presented her with the Super Scout badge.

"Congratulations!" I exclaimed. "The top-secret prize that Liberty mentioned earlier is a souvenir from any Washington, D.C., shop . . . within a budget of course."

"Oooooh, maybe a stuffed animal wearing a Washington, D.C., sweater or something like that," Freedom said with a huge smile.

I nodded, happy for her excitement.

"Fear not, secret agents," Liberty added. "Since you all completed the mission objectives, you get ice cream!"

Everybody cheered.

I said, "Great job, guys! Let's head over for a waffle cone. There is still so much to see in Washington. We can't do it all in one trip. We will have to come back."

After gathering all our items from the hotel, we boarded the Metro again, and later, the train as we journeyed back home. The Crew slept almost the whole way.

"Thank you so much, Mr. Revere," the Crew said in turn.

"Thank you all. Now don't forget to keep reading your history books, and I will see you in class after the fall break," I said, then turned to Tommy. "I will see you tomorrow at the hospital, okay?"

"Sure thing, Mr. Revere, great trip," Tommy said, softly.

The next day I woke up early and the sun was shining brightly.

"Look what I got for Tommy and his grandpa," Liberty said. In his mouth he held a T-shirt that read "Hi, I'm Bill. Bill of Rights."

I smiled. Liberty always found a way to make me laugh no matter the situation. "That's simply perfect," I said.

As we made our way back to the Veterans' Hospital entrance, the size and beauty of the American flag blowing in the slight breeze once again captured my attention. I paused for a moment while my mind crept back to Baltimore Harbor. What courage the early Americans had.

At the hospital entrance, a security guard once again gave my colonial outfit a look and handed me a visitor's badge. I slowly walked toward the elevators feeling nervousness in my stomach. I

realized I was afraid of what I might see or hear about Tommy's grandpa and what I would say to comfort Tommy. A family I recognized from the last visit passed me in the hall, looking worn-out. I stopped for moment to think of what it would be like to walk these same cold halls day after day visiting a loved one.

When I reached Tommy's grandfather's room, I quietly opened the door. As I looked in, I was pleasantly surprised to see Tommy's grandfather sitting up and engaged in conversation.

"Check this out, Grandpa," Tommy said. "I filled up the notebook you gave me! I really tried to pay attention and add things that you would find interesting. There are some cool facts about the White House and the Capitol Building, oh, and even the Washington Monument. I brought your photo with me and took pictures to go with my notes. You kinda went on the field trip to Washington, D.C., with me."

Tommy's grandfather smiled as Tommy read from the notebook aloud. "Wow, you did all this? That's fantastic. You are one lucky kid to be able to see these incredible sites."

Tommy added excitedly, "Oh, and we also got to meet Francis Scott Key in Baltimore just before he wrote the National Anthem."

Tommy's grandfather smiled broadly as Tommy continued his story. I stood in the corner and waited for him to finish.

"Yes, Grandpa. The bombs really did burst in air. The Americans had so much courage to keep fighting. I mean the odds were totally against them. They were being bombed left and right by the British. There were like a zillion British boats in the harbor but somehow the American flag was still waving when the sun came up," Tommy said, waving his arms wildly.

Tommy's grandfather listened closely with a glint in his eye.

"And the best was when we were on the deck of the ship and the flag rose and we didn't know if it was British or American," Tommy continued. "And Francis Scott Key was like, *Wow, it's the American flag, we are still free. It was really cool!*"

"Oh, now that does sound cool," Tommy's grandfather said. "You really got around DC, all the way back to 1814." Smiling widely, Tommy's grandfather leaned back on the bed. He looked tired but happy. He motioned for Tommy to sit on the end of the bed beside him.

In a deep but soft voice he said, "Tommy, we don't know how long any of us have. But remember this: You live in an incredible country where you are truly free. To dream, to speak, to believe, and to reach as far as your skills and dedication will take you. Always remember how lucky you are even if some days seem very hard."

Tommy couldn't sit still. He jumped up, smiled, and gave his grandfather a big hug.

His grandfather hugged him back and said, "Now, go on, get out of here. Go outside in the sun and practice your spiral with that magical talking horse of yours." Tommy's grandfather smiled and patted Tommy on the head. He held his hand up for a high five.

"Okay, Grandpa, get some rest, you need it," Tommy teased, gently matching his grandfather's tone. "I'll do a couple extra laps just for you." He tucked in the blanket under his grandfather's chest.

Tommy picked up his football and turned toward the door.

"Hi, Tommy," I said softly, so as not to startle him.

"Oh, hi, Mr. Revere," Tommy replied, surprised.

We walked down the hall and I put my arm around Tommy's shoulder. He looked up at me and said, "Want to go play some football? Grandpa said I need to practice my spiral."

"Great idea, Tommy. Maybe Liberty can even run some plays," I said.

We made our way back downstairs and out the sliding double doors of the main hospital entrance. This time Tommy paused and looked up at the American flag.

"My grandfather is a hero and always will be. I'll never forget what this flag and our country mean to him," he said.

I nodded, pausing in place.

We crossed over to the field and found Liberty munching away on some snacks I left for him. "Why, hellooo there," Liberty said, with his mouth full.

"Mr. Revere said you are a great wide receiver," Tommy said with a smirk.

"I am?" Liberty replied. "Um, sure I am. Except for the minor detail that I can't really catch the ball with my hooves. But no big deal, I can catch the ball in my mouth. I've been accused of having a big mouth." He cleared his throat and looked my way.

We all laughed. "Okay, never mind about receiving," Tommy said. "How about you block while Mr. Revere goes out for a pass? You would be a great offensive lineman."

"Done. Dealio. I'm the king of blocking, I own blocking, I am blocking," Liberty said, shaking his body as if he were listening to a fight song. "Now, you just have to explain to me what *blocking* is, exactly."

I smiled, shook my head, and thought, This should be interesting.

"Hut, hut, hike. Go long, Mr. Revere!" Tommy shouted.

At that moment, a gust of wind pushed the flag to its fullest size. It shook against the flagpole as if it were ready to fly off into the air.

Liberty was darting back and forth in front of Tommy, blocking imaginary players. I shook my head at a horse playing football. Only Liberty!

I made a quick fake and turn. Tommy whipped the ball my way.

When the ball reached my hands for the catch, I heard Tommy shout, "Mr. Revere, did you see that spiral?"

"Sure did, Tommy!" I said walking back to the huddle. "I know your grandfather is proud."

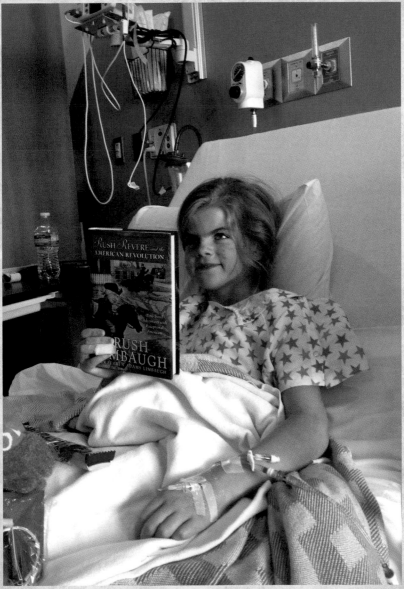

This exceptional young American named Alexia B. is a direct descendent of
Pilgrims William Bradford and Elder William Brewster.
We are very proud of her!

This young fan of the book series is proudly wearing the American flag. We love to see patriotism like this!

Acknowledgments

I could not write these books by myself. I am blessed to have an exceptional team assembled to assist me, and they each make great contributions without which these books might never be published. I am forever grateful.

My wife, Kathryn, is a coauthor and the tireless leader behind the entire series. She is the first one to get started *early* every morning and the last to wrap it in the evening. Kathryn is committed to the pursuit of excellence, and her leadership and the example she sets inspire everyone around her to be their very best. We are all very lucky: Kathryn is uncommonly intelligent and combines it with a genuine compassion and caring for so many. She has been all over the world and brings her rich, real-life experiences to every one of these books. Her goal, and ours, is to touch each reader in a genuine and heartfelt way.

Jonathan Adams Rogers is irreplaceable. He is devoted to ensuring top-quality, accurate, honest portrayals of our history. Jonathan spends countless hours behind the scenes—researching, fact-checking, editing, and collaborating. The series would simply not be the same without him.

Chris Schoebinger and Christopher Hiers are intricate parts of the team. Their hard work and wonderful talent profoundly help to bring this vision to life.

Heartfelt thank-yous go out to my brother, David Limbaugh, Penelope Rogers, Louise Burke, Mitchell Ivers, the Simon & Schuster team, and everyone who is part of the Adventures of Rush Revere "Crew." It's a great team to be on!

This Adventures Series is a labor of love with a mission to share the incredible stories of our founding in a unique and creative way. Our goal is to rekindle the patriotic spirit and encourage it to live on through the younger generations. Thank you all from the bottom of our hearts for embracing this series and providing us with the motivation to continue on. The photos, letters, and sincere praise that we receive from around the world touch our hearts beyond words. We so appreciate your support, more than you can know.

Photo Credits